ONCE UPON A MISSING TIME
A novel of alien

BY

PHILIP MANTLE

Published in 2017 by Flying Disk Press

http://flyingdiskpress.blogspot.co.uk/

Flying Disk Press
4 St Michaels Avenue
Pontefract
West Yorkshire
England
WF8 4QX

CONTENTS:

Acknowledgments:

I would like to thank fellow UFO researchers Clive Potter and Andrew Walmsley for their support and encouragement in preparing this book. I would also like to thank two of the world's most influential UFO researchers for their help and knowledge, both of whom are sadly no longer with us, Graham Birdsall and Budd Hopkins.

Without the help of Robert Snow for his proof reading skills and Steve Johnson for his editing expertise this book would not have been completed. A special thanks goes to Tanya Gray for helping me re-type the manuscript. I would also like to thank a number of close encounter witnesses in the UK who were the inspiration for this book. I am not permitted to name many of them but one that I can name is Rosalind Reynolds. Thank you Rosalind.

And last but not least I would like to thank my wife Christine for all her support and encouragement. I have sat on this manuscript for quite some time and were it not for my wife's persistence I would never have thought of publishing it. Cover design by Mark Randall.

Philip Mantle

******

INTRODUCTION

The subject of alien abductions is, without question, a controversial one. On one side of the fence, you have those that firmly believe that mankind is being visited by beings from another world that is interacting with us. On the other side, there are the skeptics who argue that such experiences are strictly earth-bound and can be explained in conventional terms. In the middle, of course, are those that have undergone these experiences in the first place, the 'abductees', as they are commonly known...

The abductee often has no one to turn to when trying to deal with these experiences. Put yourself in their shoes, who would you tell? The encounters or experiences can often be frightening, certainly bewildering and, at the very least, extremely puzzling. They can be a 'one-off', while others have a whole range of encounters lasting many years. Some abductees seek the help of UFO researchers, but many, a majority some would argue, simply keep things to themselves.

No matter which side of the fence you might be on, one thing that both camps agree upon is that the alien abduction experience does take place. The argument, of course, still rages: is the nature and origin of these experiences from inner or outer space?

What you are about to read is a work of fiction. Although it is based in the UK in 1990, it could, in reality, be anywhere in the world. Whatever is the nature and origin of the alien abduction experience, it certainly does not respect any national or international boundaries. Most, if not all, abductees undergo these experiences whilst going about their everyday tasks - walking the dog, on their way to work or simply driving home. There is no pattern to these events, they are not gender specific and they don't favour any age group, location or anything else for that matter. They seem to be totally random.

Although this is a work of fiction, the story and the characters are all based on real people and real-life events. I have changed their identities simply to protect them. The discussions and debates surrounding the nature and origin of the alien abduction experience continue and so do the encounters. More and more people still come forward looking for the answers. This book is not designed to provide any answers one way or the other; instead it serves to illustrate how ordinary people can be caught up in this extraordinary phenomenon. Whether the alien abduction takes place in inner or outer space I leave you to decide.

Philip Mantle.

******

PROLOGUE

The rural village of East Yardsley was like most other North Yorkshire villages of its time. It had its pub, shop, post office, village hall and school. The main source of income for most was farming. The hills and moors around the village were dotted with sheep farms that had been there down the generations. The lush green landscape was a patchwork of fields boarded by the iconic dry stone walls. Nothing much had changed here for decades although one small hotel had opened on the outskirts of the village which mainly catered for the small but increasing tourist trade in the area.

Britain in 1990 had just seen a change in Prime Minister with John Major replacing Margaret Thatcher. The Falklands conflict and the miners strike were consigned to the history books. Not that either of these events had any impact on village life in East Yardsley. The most talked about events here centered around who would win the prizes at the annual village fete.

This was still the era long before the home computer, the internet, smart phones and digital technology. All of these were waiting on the horizon. For the farming community, especially the sheep farmers, the price of wool was far more important than most things in their lives. It was their sheep from which they earned their living and poor wool prices and bad weather were often the topic of conversation over a pint of beer in the local pub.

Leonard Howe had farmed these hills all of his adult life. His flock of 1000 sheep were the center of his universe. His father and grandfather before him had farmed the same breed of sheep and had been born and died in the same house in which he still lived. He knew everything there was to know about sheep, or so he thought. He had lived through every type of weather that the Yorkshire Moors could throw at him and the many harsh winters he had lived through were etched on the lines of his face. Today though something was not quite right. Sheep in Britain had no natural predators with Wolves long since exterminated. These animals were still instinctively nervous and today something had put them on edge. Leonard Howe had checked for stray dogs, poachers, tourists wondering off the beaten track, everything, but he could not put his finger on why today, of all days, his flock of sheep just seemed 'different'. Perhaps it was his age he thought, he's seeing things and problems that just are not there.

The Morrison family were much like many others. Alan aged 43, was a teacher at the local high school. His wife Pamela, aged 41 was a social worker for the local authority. Their daughter Wendy was a typical thirteen year old girl interested in music and her friends and of course boys. Their family life was under pressure like a lot of families in 1990. They both worked long hours and had little time for themselves. At times it seemed that all they did was work and the pressure on their relationship was starting to tell.

This day had started like any other day for the Morrison family. A quick breakfast before the dash to work. Alan to the local high school to teach and Pamela en-route to visit a number of clients on her appointment list. That evening they had planned to visit Pamela's parents who lived a short drive away and Alan was looking forward to watching the snooker on TV. Little did they all know that today their lives would change forever?

Tonight whilst driving back from their in-laws home near the rural North Yorkshire village of East Yardsley, the Morrison family encounter something that would change their lives and world view forever. The Morrison's have a close encounter, a close encounter with something quite extraordinary. On arriving home they discover nearly four hours of their lives missing. Plagued by nightmarish dreams the Morrison's look for answers for their 'missing time'. Their search for answers threatens to tear the family apart, leaving them with lives that will never be the same again.

******

PART ONE

MISSING TIME

CHAPTER ONE

JUST ANOTHER ORDINARY DAY

A babble of excited conversation filled the classroom and spilled out into the corridor beyond. Alan Morrison hurried towards the open door as fast as the immense pile of exercise books with which he was wrestling would allow. He was tall and slim, blessed with a mass of closely-curled blonde hair which framed a kindly face possessing sharply-defined features and startling blue eyes which the passing years had not dulled. His white shirt, plain blue tie, black trousers and gleaming black shoes were all wisely chosen and tastefully matched to ease the inevitable discomfort brought on by the clammy autumn heat. As he made his way down the corridor on long, wiry legs, he caught a foot against a radiator pipe and he stumbled, nearly losing his briefcase from the top of the pile of books he carried.

Further down the corridor, a number of other teachers were peering around half-open doors, but most of the disapproving looks melted away when they saw him approaching. With a bright smile and a nod of apology, he ducked into the classroom and kicked the door shut with his heel before thankfully dumping the books on a convenient empty desk.

His entrance had gone unnoticed by all but the most attentive of the first year class and the noise of excited chatter was almost deafening with the door shut. How they could hope to hear each other, he just did not know. He took a deep breath; spread his arms wide as if in blessing and paused for a moment.

"QUIET!!"

A girl near to him turned quickly and fixed him with mischievous brown eyes as the rest of the startled class came to order. In her young face he could quite clearly see the slow birth of stunning beauty taking place and he was conscious of the fact that her strong character had already ensured her the position of class leader.

"No need to shout sir."

"How else could I make myself heard above your row, Julie?"

He flashed a quick smile at her and watched as she dropped her eyes and began to fiddle with her brightly-coloured pencil case in order to disguise her embarrassment. The girls around her hid giggles behind small hands as the rest of the class moved to their desks in a momentary crescendo of rummaging and scraping. He scanned the young faces for a moment and drew satisfaction from the looks of expectation he saw. He reached for the book on top of the pile and leafed through it until he reached the essay he had set at the end of the last lesson.

"Your homework was very good overall. It looks like some of us have very active imaginations, judging by the contributions, and I hope you can all keep this standard throughout the year."

He glanced at the name on the front of the book he held and sent it whizzing across the room towards its owner, a tall, lithe boy who leapt from his seat to catch it, to the applause of his fellows. Alan joined in the applause for a moment.

"Good catch Darren. Cricket team for you, eh?"

He began to clear the rest of the pile in the same manner and smiled at the antics, giggles and shrieks which resulted as some of the less able members of the class reached out only to find the spinning book evading their clutching hands and slithering across the floor.

Alan knew that many of his colleagues would disapprove of this behaviour, but it fitted in with the ethos of the progressive style of teaching which he had picked up at college twelve years ago and still practiced today. He found that light-hearted fun interwoven with a polished and bright teaching style seemed to make learning an enjoyable experience for all involved. The exam grades of the classes he had taught in the past added credence to the fact that it also produced better students in the long term. The only problem apparent to him was that things did get a little loud sometimes. He could live with this and also with the knowledge that others couldn't. He again held his hands out for silence.

"Okay everyone, ears open and mouths shut for a few moments. Mr. Morrison has a few words to say about the forthcoming school play and he would like all of you to take note. Firstly, all of you who are in the cast should be at the final rehearsal this lunchtime. Secondly, those of you who haven't quite made the bright lights and stardom need not despair as no show is complete without an audience so you can all come along and watch."

A chubby, red-cheeked girl seated at the back of the classroom thrust a podgy arm into the air. She spoke without waiting for acknowledgement.

"Is your Wendy going to be in the play, sir?"

The question was edged with the slightest hint of jealousy interwoven with an even less tangible hint of malice. Even he had to admit that teaching at the school which his daughter attended did make life difficult at times. Doubly so when her obvious intelligence and quick-wittedness earned her good marks and praise from all the staff in the school. He decided not to rise to the challenge.

"Yes, Naomi, Wendy will be in the play, but there was nothing stopping you auditioning for her part if you wanted to."

He grinned at her as he had at Julie in order to dilute the impact of words which could have stung and upset had they been delivered maliciously or vengefully. He saw the faintest hint of a smile at the corners of her mouth as her young mind grappled with confused feelings. Satisfied at his defusing of the situation, he broadened his attention once more to take in the rest of the class.

"Okay folks, take out your workbooks and begin a new page."

He took up chalk and wrote the word 'VERB' on the blackboard in large, hurried letters.

"That is today's title. Can anyone tell me what a verb is?"

A forest of eager young hands shot into the air and the lesson, under his coaxing direction, began to gather pace.

He allowed the class to make its noisy way out of the classroom a few minutes early. He had to be away as soon after twelve as possible and wanted to make time for the inevitable few to have their quiet words with him. Julie was one of those who stayed behind and detained him with her attentions which, given a few more years, may have been worrying. They were, at the moment, merely flattering. Their conversation was such that he knew it would not conclude until she had been allowed to carry his briefcase out to the car and deposit it on the back seat.

As they walked through the exit doors and out into the playground, he was momentarily dazzled by the bright autumn sun which shone from a cloudless sky the colour of blue pen ink and broke into the cocoon of subdued calm and dim coolness which the school corridors had woven around them both. He shielded his eyes with a hand and took a quick look around the crowded playground for any signs of brewing trouble amongst the disorganised games which had sprung up under the bright sun before turning towards the car park. Julie lugged his suitcase along heroically, the effort not stilling her enthusiastic chatter.

"Do you think the play will go off alright, sir?"

He squinted at her as he spoke.

"I don't see why not, but then that's up to you isn't it, Julie? You will be at the rehearsal this lunchtime won't you? Twelve-fifteen prompt."

"Yes, sir. It's just… well it's just that I'm a bit nervous. You see, Naomi says that people laugh when you make mistakes."

He laughed himself.

"Then Naomi's wrong about that. I don't think the people there will be looking out for mistakes, they'll just be enjoying the play."

"I know, sir, but Naomi and Jane are coming and they said that they'd tell everyone if I made a mistake."

They reached his dark blue Passat and he paused to unlock the doors before replying. He made an effort to reassure Julie.

"If Naomi and her friends say anything to you about your acting then tell them to come and see me about their problems. They aren't even in the play so how can they criticise you?"

She heaved his suitcase onto the car's back seat with a grunt of exertion.

"Yes, sir, but they said!"

"Naomi and Jane won't say a word. I promise you."

Julie appeared satisfied, if still slightly nervous. He understood how she felt. He had seen this all before: the slower ones picking on the bright ones out of jealousy and insecurity. He considered that differences of this nature should be reconciled as soon as possible and made a mental note to speak to Naomi and her friends about this. Julie opened her mouth to continue, but Alan stemmed any further worries.

"Everything will be fine, Julie. Now it's time you were getting to that rehearsal. Don't forget that you have to get changed as well."

"Yes, sir."

She turned and ran back towards the playground. He worried about her for a moment before mentally reassuring himself. He would sort things out later. Now he had to meet Pamela and he had a feeling that he was already late. He was just about to twist the key in the ignition when a shout made him look up.

Brian Wilcox was obviously not a man whose first priority in life was tidiness. His battered trainers, roomy slacks and ageing shirt were the only clothes he ever wore to school and Alan sometimes wondered if he had a whole wardrobe composed solely of throw-outs and seconds. As he sauntered up to him, friendly smile on his round face, he thrust one hand deep into a pocket and used the other to try and put some order into the long black hair to which the warm autumn breeze was giving vigorous life.

"You not at the rehearsal, Alan?"

"Can't today, Brian, I've got to meet Pamela."

Brian ended the tussle with his hair and deposited the other hand in his trouser pocket.

"Too bad, things seem to be working out well. They're a good bunch, that lot, especially your Wendy."

Alan was conscious that he was late, but Brian was one of the few people he would be late for. They had joined the school at the same time and Alan had taken an instant liking to his endearingly haphazard ways and quick wit. Brian was a man without prejudices, cares or narrow-minded opinions and Alan admired and respected him for that. He was also a good friend and colleague and they spent a great deal of time together outside of school. Brian's next question was posed with his certain brand of friendly concern, which was neither prying nor aloof.

"You and Pam sorted things out yet anyway?"

Alan frowned slightly.

"Not really. We both need more time together, but what with her job and this play we haven't had much time for anything other than eating together lately. She's so damned tired when it gets to around nine that I can't get any sense out of her at all."

The concern on Brian's face deepened.

"You should talk to her when you see her now. Don't let this thing get out of hand or you could both suffer."

He knew this and had anyone other than Brian pointed it out to him, then he would have no doubt found a polite way of telling them to mind their own damned business. But there was something about Brian's unselfish concern for his relationship with Pamela which hardened his own resolve to sort things out. He was about to reply when a shout drew their attentions to the school's main entrance. They both instantly recognised the tweed cape and dark yellow cardigan of Sydney Potter, the school's head and a man old in both body and mind. Brian raised his eyebrows and smiled, but did not turn away from Alan.

"Looks like it's me who gets hung this dinnertime."

The shout rang out again, louder and more strident this time.

"Have to go, Alan. Look, don't forget about what I've said. I'll see you tonight at the play."

Brian smiled and then turned and ambled off in the headmaster's general direction, authority not quickening his pace in the slightest. Alan smiled to himself and turned the ignition key. The Passat's throaty engine roared into life and he eased the car slowly out of the car park, picking up speed once he was out on the narrow road leading into the town.

******

CHAPTER TWO

LATE FOR LUNCH

As he drove into the centre of the village and manoeuvred the large car into the crowded pub car park, Alan caught sight of Pamela at one of the tables set up on the small, well-cut green behind the rustic pub bearing the sign 'The Rope and Anchor'. Her gaze told him that he was even later than she had been. He braced himself, counted to ten, and got out of the car. He left the window down and the door unlocked, not fearing the theft of his own car from the park of a pub he had been frequenting since the age of seventeen. He pecked Pamela on the forehead as he sat down on the seat facing her and folded his elbows on the table.

She turned her deep brown eyes on him and fixed him with a penetrating gaze for a moment before averting them and staring once more at the polished pine of the table.

"You're late."

He reached out and took one of her small, slender hands in his.

"Sorry, I had to finish organising the play."

She tried to pull her hand away, but he held her wrist gently yet firmly. With his other hand he stroked her chin and neck until she looked at him again.

Her slim face held delicately-formed features which were stunningly beautiful to him. She possessed poise and grace of movement which sometimes made him stop and stare in wonder. At the moment, she was frowning and her displeased countenance looked as if it was there to stay for the time being.

"I've had a bad morning and I expected you to be on time. Andrew decided that he was going to take lunch with me and I've had to keep him happy for the past fifteen minutes."

As if on cue, Andrew Gibson swept through the open door of the pub carrying a gin and tonic and a pint of bitter. He was a short, slightly-built man with a beard the same colour as his mousy crew-cut hair. He had a lean, pale face which bore sharply-chiselled, yet strangely unattractive, features and a protruding chin, which the beard accentuated rather than disguised. His inflated self-appraisal and accompanying lack of self-awareness were made acutely obvious by the excessive amount of gold accessories with which he adorned his expensive suit. The open neck of his shirt revealed a short, oversized gold chain from which hung a small steel plate bearing the legend – 'RED HOT'.

Pamela glanced behind her and grimaced privately at his approach. He sat too close to her and eyed Alan coolly.

"I didn't know we were going to have company. What are you having, Alan?"

He recognised Gibson's condescending charm and countered it effortlessly.

"Nothing thanks. I only dropped by to discuss a few things with Pamela. I have to be getting back to school in a few minutes."

He chose to ignore the message veiled behind Alan's words and began an attempt to discuss the morning's work with Pamela. She shot a pleading look across the table which Gibson missed, but which Alan interpreted clearly.

"Do you have anything planned for tonight, Pamela?"

She turned gratefully back to Alan and spoke to Gibson without looking at him.

"Sorry, Andrew, but we have to make some plans for the evening. Can we talk about this back at work?"

Gibson frowned for a moment before muttering a 'sure' and standing up. In a last-minute attempt to regain control of the situation, which he felt was slipping through his fingers, he turned to Alan.

"See you later, Alan. I hope you both have a nice evening."

Alan gave him a ridiculously broad and deliberately insincere smile which deflected and negated the challenge which he had issued.

"Thanks, Andrew, we will."

Gibson knew that he was not going to get anywhere today. His plan to corner Pamela and bestow affections upon her for the entire duration of their lunch hour had been disrupted and his attempts to subdue Alan had failed miserably. He scanned the small beer garden thoughtfully for a second before heading back into the pub. Alan and Pamela joined hands over the table again. Their mutual relief at Gibson's departure had raised the general mood of their meeting and Alan took the initiative.

"You know that the play is tonight? Well, I was thinking that I could pick you up at around twenty past five and we could go and get something to eat in the village before going back to the school. That lot should wind up around half past eight. Then we could go home and pack Wendy off to bed and then talk for a while."

He looked to her for a reply and saw that a wave of sorrow had washed over her face and drowned her happy smile. It seemed as if the sky above darkened for a second and he already knew what she was going to say.

"I'm sorry, Alan. Janice and I have to work late tonight. They're introducing new counselling techniques next month and it's important that we know just what's involved so as we can identify problems now."

He felt his own pleasant mood slipping away and slowly dissolving in the frustration which arose within him. He was tired of feeling this way.

"But this is important, Pamela. You know that Wendy's playing one of the lead parts. She needs to know that we are both there. Can't you stop pushing yourself for just one night and let everything go? It is Friday night after all. What's wrong with Monday?"

She pulled her hand away from his and her expression and words became sterner and more laconic.

"There won't be any time, Alan. Janice is on holiday tomorrow and I'll have all her paperwork to do on Monday."

Alan felt as if he was falling once more into a familiar groove and one which he had come to hate over the last few months. He knew that Pamela was aware of the problems which existed between them, but now he was seeing the side of her which chose to be ignorant of everything except her work, to which her devotion was becoming almost absolute. He resented this devotion, not just because it meant that he never saw her, but also because he knew that it was her way of hiding from a truth which she perceived to be potentially damaging to their relationship. He knew that he would never get through to her until she changed her attitude. He wanted to shout at her, to tell her how he felt and that he loved her and cared for her. He wanted to hold her, but he was aware that the setting and the mood which had settled on them both would not tolerate such an emotional outburst. From an early age he had held the belief that true love could ride all emotional storms and emerge strongly and gracefully from all the disagreements and arguments which battered it. Now he felt a

little naive as he felt the foundations of his own love for Pamela shaking ever so slightly.

"Okay, we'll be fine for tonight. Do you want me to pick you up after the play?"

She smiled again.

"About quarter to nine outside the post office should be fine. Oh, and can we stop by at mum and dad's on the way home? There's an old people's get together at the community centre next week and I'd like to get them there. It'll give Val a chance to get out with her mates as well."

Alan knew that arguing over this minor point could upset things still further.

"Okay, but I don't want to stop too long."

"We won't, just long enough for me to get things sorted out with them."

She saw that groups of people were standing around them preparing to leave. She glanced at her own watch and frowned at it then stood and pecked Alan on the forehead.

"Got to go. I'm late as it is. See you tonight."

"Yeah, see you tonight."

He watched her slender form retreat across the grass. As she walked through the car park, he crossed the small garden and entered the dim coolness of the fast-emptying pub. It was charmingly rustic, the dark oak booths, low roof timbers and shining horse brasses were all solid and genuine, not the product of an idealistic brewery designer's pen. He ordered a pint of bitter and drank it slowly in the corner booth, which still bore the initials he had scratched into its hard body over twenty years ago.

After emptying his glass, he drove back to school deep in thought.

******

CHAPTER THREE

A FACE IN THE MIST

The afternoon heralded last minute measures for the play and the speed at which it passed amazed even Alan. Finally, with buttons sewn on, lines re-written, scenery corrected and tears mopped up, preparations were complete.

He went into the village for a meal at the pub, but was back by 6pm, by which time the hall was filling with parents and children. He saw Naomi and her charmed group sitting together near the back and remembered Julie's words. Making a conscious effort to keep a low profile, he approached them and spoke quietly for a few moments. Once satisfied that he had made them see reason, he walked back along the side of the hall and around the side of the stage to take up his discreet position in the wings, where he could be called upon if required.

To him, it seemed that the countless hours of preparation which had gone into the play had all been worthwhile as the cast stood in the glare of the limelights at the end and bowed repeatedly at the audience's enthusiastic applause. The school hall lost its usual drab character for a fleeting moment and became a place of colourful shining lights and happiness with the stage becoming a window through which a fantastic world of inspiration and imagination could be glimpsed. The illusion died only slowly as the applause gradually faded and people in the audience began collecting bags and putting on jackets.

Alan was still slightly high on the atmosphere which the production had woven around him as Wendy approached him. She was unusually tall for her age and had inherited Pamela's slender figure, which, in time, was obviously destined to become as shapely as her mother's. Her features were as sharp and proud as Alan's, her oval face a faithful copy of her mother's and her eyes a striking shade of green. Her hair flowed down over her shoulders in a shining auburn river of flowing curls. To Alan she was the most beautiful child he had ever seen and she was a lasting, growing symbol of his love for Pamela. When she spoke her voice was deeper, cultured and mellower than would have been expected for a twelve year-old girl.

"What did you think, dad?"

He knocked the end of her nose with his knuckle and smiled lovingly at her.

"You were very good, Wendy. You were all brilliant. I've got to admit it, I'm impressed."

His praise broadened her smile. He looked steadily at her for a moment before her head snapped round. Julie had prodded her in the back.

"Come on, Wendy, we've got to get changed!"

With a last look at her father, Wendy and Julie made their way down the corridor, laughing and shrieking, to the classroom at its end, which had been turned into a makeshift dressing room. Alan poked his head around the corner and scanned the emptying hall of familiar faces, but saw none. He secretly hoped that Pamela had had second thoughts and decided to come along anyway. Of her, he saw no sign. A sharp prod in the back made him turn round. He saw Brian brandishing a vicious-looking scimitar which glistened in the stage lights.

"Your money or your life, Morrison!"

Alan laughed when he recognised the cardboard and tinfoil prop which had been used during the play's only fight scene. Still laughing, he thrust his hands into the air and backed into the wings.

"Don't shoot, I'll do anything," he cried in a shrill falsetto voice.

Brian's mirth surfaced and they both began to laugh, letting the pressures of the day slip away. When their laughter had subsided, Brian stepped onto the stage and looked out on the now-empty hall.

"Good turnout wasn't it, Alan?"

"Yeah, not bad. Did we break even?"

Alan went to the lighting console and began to shut off the power to the stage and hall lights. He left the footlights burning and joined Brian, who was consulting a small black notebook.

"I think so. According to this, we may have made a profit."

"Does that mean that we get our classrooms painted?"

Brian gave him a pained look.

"You're joking, aren't you?"

"I wish I wasn't. I've never known a time when this school was so seriously under-funded. How do they expect us to turn out tomorrow's Einstein's if we can't afford to buy blackboard chalk?"

Brian pursed his lips and shrugged.

"Don't ask me. Perhaps they should have trained us in alchemy at college. You know, turning gold into base metals and that kind of thing."

"That's base things into gold, by the way, Brian."

"Nope, that's an indictment of our whole education system, Alan."

They both laughed for a few moments before Wendy's voice attracted their attention.

"Hi, Mr. Wilcox!"

Brian turned to her and wielded the scimitar in a threatening manner.

"Don't come any closer! Be gone outsider!"

Wendy began to giggle uncontrollably and Alan turned to the backstage exit.

"Yep, I think we'd better both be gone to bed. I don't know about you kid, but I've had a hard day. You going out tomorrow, Brian?"

"I'll be in the pub with Caroline in the evening. I somehow don't think that the kids will want to be seen out with us nowadays, so they won't be there."

Alan nodded.

"Yeah, I know what you mean. If I can manage to drag Pamela away from her work, we may well end up there as well."

Brian waved at them as they went through the exit and shouted after them.

"Okay, see you tomorrow. Monday if you don't make it!"

They stepped out into the warm night and headed for the Passat. Wendy babbled excitedly about the play and Alan contented her by agreeing or disagreeing with what she said, even though his mind was concerned with Pamela.

Once away from the car park and out onto the road, he glanced at the car's clock – eight-forty. He could make the village in five minutes if he pushed it. He increased pressure on the accelerator and the big car responded smoothly, the speedometer reaching fifty quickly. Alan held it there and concentrated on negotiating the frequent sharp bends in the road.

He reached the post office with a minute to spare and found Pamela waiting for him in the doorway. Wendy greeted her mother jubilantly and Pamela was careful

to listen to everything she had to tell her about the play as Alan took the left fork at the 'Rope & Anchor' and followed the road up the side of the hill to her parents' house. He was acutely conscious of the fact that she had not spoken to him, but he was also determined to make her break the ice. Tonight, he resolved, they would get to the bottom of whatever had been troubling them. He was weary of this cold, uncommunicative silence.

The car's headlights illuminated the small row of cottages nestling into the side of the hill, beyond which unfolded the glittering amber vistas of widely-spaced town and cities. He brought the car to a gentle halt outside the first house of the low and isolated terrace in which Pamela had been born and brought up. Pamela shouted as they entered the small hall and almost immediately a door at its far end opened and warm light spilled from the aperture. Valerie walked out into the hall and Pamela embraced her sister for a moment. When seen together, the contrasts were obvious. Pamela was tall and slender; Valerie was larger in frame, shorter and rounder, but still possessing the well-proportioned figure which was obviously a family characteristic. Her face was larger then Pamela's, though the features were still sharp and proud and her brown eyes danced happily.

Even though she wore only age-faded denim jeans and a baggy woollen sweater, it was still obvious that she still took pride in her appearance, despite being out of work with no prospect of employment in the future.

Alan had never been attracted to her as he had to Pamela, but Valerie had spent a great deal of time with them whilst they were courting and she and Alan had struck up a friendship which had lasted over the fifteen years of their marriage. Many times when he and Pamela had argued, Valerie had become the mediator and he was sure that her actions had closed rifts which could have developed in their marriage had the differences been allowed to go unreconciled. He couldn't help wondering that perhaps Valerie could work some of her diplomatic magic on her sister tonight. To him it looked as if they needed it.

She ushered them into the small living room which was tastefully decorated in subtle pastel shades. These were softened even further by the subdued lighting which created a warm atmosphere of calmness subconsciously woven by Pamela's parents as they aged.

Albert and Margaret Kelly were seated on armchairs in two of the room's corners facing the television which had been turned off at their arrival.

Albert Kelly was a magnificent figure of a man. Over six feet in height and massively built with an impressive mane of precisely-styled, silver hair, which showed no sign of thinning or retreating. His face looked as if it had been chipped from granite by an accomplished sculptor and his masculinity had enhanced the family's proud features. He was clean-shaven with the exception of a precisely-trimmed moustache, which was of the same grey as his sharp and clear eyes and gave the impression of seeing more than was immediately apparent. Despite the fact that he had retired from the police force as a sergeant three years before, the clothes he wore still resembled a form of casual uniform, which seemed to be missing only the black tie and heavy uniform jacket. He stood as they entered and gave Alan the same crushing handshake, which had not altered in the slightest over all the years for which he had known him. After all of those years Alan still could still not work out whether he actually liked this imposing figure, or whether he just gave him the respect which he appeared to command from all around him.

Margaret Kelly remained seated, the aluminium walking frame by her chair volunteering an impassive apology for her and also serving as a constant reminder of the crippling stroke which had struck her down days after her sixtieth birthday only two years ago. Though her body was clearly beginning to lose its vigour, it was not difficult to see in her the same shapely, slender figure and pixie-like face which Pamela had inherited. This face still held a healthy glow, though, and the shining eyes dispelled the impression that her brain might have been crippled along with her body. It was apparent, from the many trophies proudly displayed in the small wall unit opposite the fireplace, that Albert Kelly favoured more practical pursuits. He had played in both the police football team and the local amateur rugby team and his performance on the latter field had earned him quite a reputation. It was not difficult to imagine why. As Alan made small talk with Albert, he was aware that he certainly wouldn't want to be the man who had to stop sixteen flying stones of supremely fit oncoming police sergeant. He had often felt a pang of sympathy for those to whom the job had fallen.

The atmosphere mellowed as Valerie brought the tea in and they immediately began to relax in the familiar surroundings. Very soon, the room was brightened with conversation and laughter. Alan's attention was drawn by Albert's snooker talk, a sport for which the man's enthusiasm had grown since he had had more time to both play and watch it. Alan also enjoyed the calming effect which snooker had on his oft-frayed nerves, but Pamela despised the sport, so he would never admit to this. He glanced over to the corner of the room and saw Pamela seated on a stool, leaning towards her mother and obviously deep in conversation. He could feel his chances of sorting things out slipping away into the autumn evening. As a form of self-comfort, he began to plan the rest of the evening around the snooker final and was careful to extract from Albert's enthusiastic conversation the start time of the semi-final: 10pm. He snatched a quick glance at his watch and performed some rapid mental arithmetic. To catch it, they would have to be leaving pretty soon.

He drained his tea mug, declined Albert's offer of a refill and took a quick glance round the room. His eyes settled on his daughter who was seated on the couch facing the fireplace. He managed to catch Pamela's eyes and directed her to their sleeping daughter. She gave him an exasperated look, but nodded quickly. Margaret had noticed the unheard conversation between them and was quick to act, curtailing her conversation with Pamela politely and looking at Albert.

"Albert, could you help me get into bed in a little while? I'm feeling tired and I don't think I can face any more snooker today."

Albert Kelly had approached his wife's disability in the same calm and unemotional way he had approached all the other problems which he had encountered in his life. To people outside the family, it appeared that he was almost indifferent to his wife's suffering, but to a close relative and those others to whom he chose to speak his feelings, it was clear that he took great pride in looking after his wife. He had made sure that the transition to the new life which had been suddenly thrust upon her was as painless as possible.

Alan had seen the way the big man lifted her easily and carefully from her chair and supported her with one hand whilst he moved the walking frame to within her grasp, he had seen him go running when she had fallen and he had fleetingly glimpsed the intense sorrow and frustration which Albert felt when he helped her back onto her near-useless feet.

He stood now and watched as Albert picked his wife up and cradled her in his arms. This journey could not be made with the walking frame as the stairs proved insurmountable nowadays, even with the impassive and paradoxically encumbering support which it provide. Once her body was clear of the chair, he lowered her gently to the ground and supported her in a standing position as she said her sheepish, yet oddly sad, goodbyes. They moved aside as Albert lifted his wife once more and carried her carefully through the door. They heard carefully placed feet ascend the stairway and then a heavy silence descended upon the room. Pamela was the first to speak and her deep voice seemed to break an age of stuffy silence.

"I'll just go and help dad and then we can go home, Alan. Wendy looks dead beat."

He smiled and nodded his agreement as she swept out of the room. He stared for a moment at Wendy's form on the couch, features peacefully and beautifully composed in a soft sleep, before the sounds of clacking pottery mixed with a static-laden radio station floated through the open kitchen door. He went into the brightly-decorated kitchen and dried the tea mugs despite Valerie's half-hearted protests. They made small talk for a while, before she turned to the subject which lay on their minds.

"There's no point trying to hide it, Alan. I know that Pamela and you have had a tiff. The only thing which amazes me is that she didn't tell me about it herself."

Alan saw no point in hiding the truth from her, or from himself.

"Yeah, things aren't too good at the moment. I've been organising the school play for a month and Pam never seems to finish work much before 8pm these days. To be honest, I think it's just a lack of communication."

Valerie turned to him with her hands still in the washing-up bowl.

"Have you tried talking to her about this?"

"She doesn't seem to want to talk about anything nowadays. Half of the time, she's behaving as if I'm not there and the rest is taken up with mediocre conversation. I can't seem to shake the feeling that something is slipping away."

She continued to wash plates and saucers, as if this simple, manual task could focus her objectivity and prevent her feelings for Alan and her sister taking control of the conversation.

"Alan, you're both getting older. Things around you have changed and you two have been too wrapped up in your careers to notice. Take Wendy as an example, she's not going to be a child for much longer. Pretty soon she's going to need a mum and dad and if you two aren't there for her, she's going to be the one to start slipping away."

She was making more sense than Alan could have believed possible. He felt as if coherent thoughts were beginning to flow through the rivers of his mind again after what seemed an age of drought. Doubts still troubled him though.

"What can I do if she won't talk to me?"

Valerie washed the last pot, dried her hands and poured the bowl of clouded water down the drain.

"At least when she isn't talking, she's listening. I know her, Alan, she won't talk unless she can see a point to doing so, but she'll always listen, even though it doesn't seem like that sometimes. Pamela's a lot like dad in that respect."

"But how can I make sense?"

Valerie considered this question for a moment before turning to Alan with a slightly apologetic look on her face. Her voice had a wistful edge to it.

"I don't know. I'm not as close to Pamela as I used to be and it's getting more difficult to understand her as we get older."

They heard two sets of footfalls on the stairs. Valerie ended the conversation. Alan continued to dry the pots as Pamela and her father came back into the living room. Wendy awoke as they entered, but was still subdued with tiredness and contented herself with giving her attentive grandfather an abridged account of the school play. They walked back into the room and Alan saw Valerie and Pamela exchange brief glances; Pamela's was loaded with something which he preferred not to contemplate. He was counting on Valerie to defuse a situation, but he found himself another unexpectedly tactful and considerate ally. He had underestimated Albert's observational abilities. The huge man stood and gave him a quick look of reassurance which said more than a thousand words before heading for the kitchen, addressing all as he did so.

"Best place for that one is bed. We'd planned to have my brother over for tea last night, but he couldn't get here which means I've a bottle of wine which isn't going to get drunk. You two may as well have that." He opened the fridge and scanned its interior for a moment before extracting the bottle and handing it to Alan with a wink. Without waiting for a response he continued. "You two don't look like you've slept in ages, so get a bit of that down you then get to bed. Don't worry about the snooker, Alan, I'll record it and you can watch it any time."

Alan was taken aback by this unexpected display of kindness.

"You sure you want to do this, Albert? This isn't cheap stuff you know."

Albert lowered himself into an armchair.

"You know we don't drink a great deal. Go on, you're doing us a favour."

Wendy had stood up and was hanging heavily on her mother's hand. Pamela finalised matters.

"You'll have to let us have you over to dinner one night, dad. Perhaps after you've been to the community centre next Thursday?"

Albert pursed his lips in consideration for a moment and then nodded slowly.

"We could do that. How about if I phone you tomorrow?"

Pamela smiled warmly at her father and reached over to embrace him with one arm.

"Okay, thanks a lot, dad. We'll probably drop by tomorrow."

Alan moved to join his wife as they left the living room, but found that he couldn't escape Albert's crushing handshake, though he was not as worried as he could have been. He was surprised to find a friend in such an unusual place, but was most grateful for the unexpected. He looked into Albert's clear grey eyes as he spoke.

"Perhaps we could go out for a pint some time?"

"Aye, I think I could run to that, Alan. Just give me a ring. Now get off home, the both of you, you're all beginning to look done in. Don't forget, Alan, snooker at ten."

He looked at his watch. Nine thirty-five. Now he would see whether the four-figure sum he had splashed out for the Passat's overhead camshafts, multiple valves and fuel injection system would be worthwhile. He made a point of checking that all seat belts were fastened before he got into the car himself. Albert leant on the sill of Alan's open window and looked at the car's interior approvingly.

"Clever buggers, these Germans. Now don't you go breaking any speed limits!"

Another quick knowing wink. Alan knew that Albert was being deliberately hypocritical, as he had also loved to open a car up in his younger days and he still drove and handled a capable Audi 80. That also meant that there wouldn't be any speed traps over the five mile distance to the small estate where they lived. He grinned back.

"No chance. It's me driving remember?"

Albert straightened up with a broad grin and tapped the car's roof. Alan started the engine and began to reverse into the house's small driveway. He gave Albert a wave as he completed his manoeuvre and set off back down the road.

Once away from the houses and heading downhill, he increased pressure on the accelerator pedal slightly and felt the big car surge forward. Pamela gave him a look which was vaguely disapproving, but also tolerant of his wish to get home quickly. They passed The Rope and Anchor and rejoined the main road. Just as the car was moving away from the junction, Wendy's shout drew their attention.

"Look mum, a shooting star!"

They both followed her outstretched finger to point just above the hills to the north, where a small, bright white light followed a fast, steep trajectory towards the shadowy horizon. Just as it seemed that it would be lost forever behind the stark hills, it levelled out and followed the terrain for a short while before finally disappearing below the skyline at a shallower angle. They watched for a short while, puzzled, before Alan moved away from the junction and applied the power again. Pamela looked across at him once more when the speedometer reached sixty.

"Watch it, Alan."

He nodded and backed the power off a little in order to round a bend. He was preparing to accelerate again when his eyes widened and his reflexes took over for just long enough to ensure their safety, snatching his foot from the accelerator and jamming it on the brake pedal.

The car's nose dipped as the updated brakes did their work and their speed dropped rapidly until they were at a standstill. Alan took the car out of gear and applied the handbrake as he stared at the impenetrable bank of glowing green mist before them. The lights on the panel of the radio flickered into darkness and the sound from its speakers suddenly ceased. With a baffled look at Pamela he knocked the gear shift back into 'D' and moved off cautiously.

He had heard of small banks of mist in country lanes which collected in the fields and then obscured an area of road for a short while before either moving on or diffusing, but had never seen or heard of green mist. He thought of mysterious agricultural chemicals and rolled his window up quickly as he drove on slowly. He was about to remark on the fog's strangeness when a childlike scream of pure terror made them both look round. Wendy was sitting in the centre of the rear seat, as far away from either window as possible and pointing, dumbfounded, towards her left. Pamela looked round for a moment before turning back to Wendy.

"What is it, darling? What's wrong?"

Wendy continued to point at the window against which the mist pressed.

"Th... Th... There was a face there. Like a cat with funny eyes."

Pamela looked back to Alan for a moment with a concerned look on her face. She mouthed 'KEEP GOING' at him before turning back to Wendy.

"It was probably just a sheep. Maybe there's a fence down somewhere along the road."

"It didn't look like a sheep; it had no nose and funny eyes."

"It's just the fog love. It makes things look strange."

Pamela's last word seemed to echo through the air between them for a long time before there was a heavy bump which caused the car to veer across the road. Immediately, the headlights were cutting through the mist and then they were out of it and back on the familiar stretch of road again. Alan began to accelerate and took a quick look at Wendy. He was surprised to see that she was asleep again. Pamela was lying back in her seat and gazing at the sky through the sunroof. She turned back to Alan as she felt the car accelerate.

"What the hell do you think that was?"

"I don't know - some kind of fog?"

"What sort of fog is green?"

"I've told you, I don't know. But we're out of it now. Don't worry."

Contented with Wendy's safety, Pamela returned to her stargazing. Alan was reassured by the calm atmosphere which had descended upon the car's interior so soon after their journey through the strange mist, but he was also baffled by its oddly artificial nature. He accelerated sharply out of the next bend in the road and concentrated on holding the car steady on the black ribbon which curled steadily away into the unlit blackness.

As Alan swung the car into the narrow road leading to the cluster of semi-detached houses at the top of the tree-lined cul-de-sac, he recalled once more his plans for the rest of the evening. He glanced at the rear-view mirror and was reassured when he saw that Wendy was still asleep, her features composed peacefully and her breathing steady. As soon as she was indoors she would probably be asleep again and that would give him and Pamela enough time to open the wine and cover some ground.

The house's spotlight clicked into life as he brought the car to a halt at the top of the drive and it was then that he noticed the strange darkness in the cul-de-sac. All of the houses stood like dark sentinels displaying no lights whatsoever. As he left the car, he noticed that a peace, unusual for the hour, lay upon the area.

He felt strangely drained and tired as he walked to the house and unlocked the door. He noticed that Pamela was also leaning heavily against the car for balance after standing up. Wendy was also stirring. Alan smiled as she struggled childishly with the door lock for a moment before finally defeating its mechanism and slamming the door behind her in disgust as she also left the car. Alan flicked on the kitchen lights while Pamela escorted Wendy gently but firmly to her room. He deposited the wine in the fridge before dimming the lights in the living room and flopping down in his chair.

He took a pot-shot at the TV with the remote control unit. His eyes narrowed in surprise as he was greeted by a rapidly brightening collage of ever-changing monochromatic confusion. He flicked through the other channels and was greeted by the same greyness. He rose and squatted down in front of the television set, altering and resetting various controls without result before he checked the aerial link between the set and the video cassette recorder. He was dismayed to find it intact. As a last resort, he tightened all the connections before examining the video recorder. His eyes drifted slowly over its black fascia before they came to rest on the glowing digital clock.

Now his eyes widened and his eyebrows arched in one fluid movement of disbelief. The display read 01:35. He hurried to the back of the room and turned off the dimmer, dispelling the shadows which it had created, and looked at the elegant carriage clock on the mantelpiece. Its finely-crafted hands agreed impassively with its counterpart's green display and he was even more amazed to find that his watch also told the same story. He wasn't aware of Pamela entering the room, but started at her gentle touch on his arm.

"What's wrong with you?"

He pointed towards the television.

"Look at the time."

She shrugged.

"So there's been a power cut. We can soon put that right."

Alan took hold of her arm as she moved towards the VCR and pointed to the carriage clock. He also drew back his shirt cuff to reveal his own watch.

"There's nothing wrong with the video, Pam, its one thirty-five in the morning."

Pamela slowly raised her arm and scrutinised her own watch in amazement and growing consternation. She lifted the phone receiver from its rest by the TV and began to dial a number. Alan rested his hands on her shoulders and watched as her fingers tapped out the remaining digits.

"Who are you ringing?"

"The police. They'll know what's gone wrong. This must have happened to everyone else."

Alan remembered the bump just prior to leaving the mist. With a start, he realised that he may have hit a stray animal of some kind. He began to piece together the journey's strange events and realised that he may well have hit the sheep which Wendy had seen in the mist. He tapped her shoulder as the connection was made and the phone at the other end began to ring.

"Better ask them if they've had any reports of injured sheep. I think I may have hit one in the mist."

She looked around at him with bewildered and worried eyes.

"Okay, I'll see what they say. You'd better go and check the car over."

"Yeah, after this."

The receiver was lifted and a distant voice answered. Pamela composed herself before speaking.

"Hello. My name's Mrs Morrison. Could you possibly tell me if you have had any reports of injured animals in the area tonight? I think we hit something on the road just past The Rope and Anchor Inn".

There was a moment's silence before the desk officer returned to the phone.

"No, we've no reports of injured animals and no reports of any strays. Did you stop?"

"No, we were in a fog bank at the time so we couldn't see a thing. When it began to clear there was nothing on the road, so we thought it may have made its way back into the field again."

"I see. Well, if we come across anything, we'll contact you, Mrs Morrison."

"Thanks. Could you also tell me the time please?"

The officer at the other end of the line laughed.

"If you want to know the time ask a policeman, eh? Well, it's one thirty-nine exactly, Mrs Morrison."

Pamela remained silent until he spoke again.

"Hello? Are you there Mrs Morrison?"

"Er, yes, thanks a lot."

She replaced the receiver in its cradle and turned to Alan, who had heard both sides of the conversation. Their eyes met for a moment in frightened questioning before he turned away and nearly ran from the room. When she caught up with him, he was examining the car by torchlight. She leant over his shoulder as he slowly moved around the vehicle. Upon completion of his search, he snapped off the torch and straightened up slowly.

"See anything?" asked Pamela.

He shook his head.

"Not a thing. If we'd hit something, it should have left a mark of some kind."

"Perhaps we ran over something?"

He shrugged his shoulders.

"Maybe. I can't see any damage on the underside of the car, though."

An unexpectedly chilly breeze rose, causing them both to shiver involuntarily. With a last look at the car, they returned to the warmth and light of the house. Alan grabbed the wine from the fridge as Pamela locked the door. He went through into the living room and opened the drinks cabinet. As he reached in to take out the glasses, he spotted a forgotten bottle of Bell's whisky. He hastily withdrew it and poured himself a generous measure with slightly unsteady hands. Without putting the bottle down, he drained his glass and refilled it. He was about to put the top back when Pamela's voice floated through from the kitchen.

"Not so fast, I'll have one of those as well."

He filled the other glass and topped his one up before finally sealing the bottle and returning it to the cabinet. Pamela took her drink and sat down heavily on the sofa, shoulders hunched and head down. She shivered slightly for a moment and coughed as the whiskey caught her throat.

"What time did we leave my parent's house, Alan?"

"It must have been just before ten, because your dad reminded me about the snooker."

"Are you absolutely sure about that? Couldn't it have got late without us realising?"

He toyed with the idea for the sake of objectivity, but was constantly aware that it was a woefully inadequate explanation for the strange circumstances which had befallen them. He began to speak, but Pamela cut him off sharply.

"Or could you have driven slowly without realising it?"

He shook his head in a decisive manner.

"No way. We'd have had to be crawling to take this long to get home. Look, all we can do now is go to bed and check things out with your mum and dad tomorrow. There's got to be some simple explanation for all of this."

Pamela finished her drink and grimaced as the whiskey caught her throat again. She rubbed her eyes in an effort to keep awake and cupped her hands around her empty glass as she looked up at Alan.

"Maybe you're right. I'm so tired, I can't think straight."

He rose and took her glass from her, helping her from the sofa as he did so. He had to drop the glass and support her dead weight with both arms as she lost her balance for a moment and fell heavily upon him. He held her by the shoulders until she could stand unaided.

"You okay now?"

She nodded her head.

"Yeah. Must've stood up a bit too quick."

He retrieved the empty glass from the floor.

"Or a bit too much of this? Come on, let's go to bed."

He held an arm around her shoulders as they tramped up the seemingly endless staircase. To him this was merely a supporting gesture, but to her it was protecting and comforting. She felt tired, sick and strangely lonely and was glad of Alan's solid presence. She moved closer to him as he paused to check on Wendy. He smiled for a moment at the bundle of covers from which emanated the sound of steady and slow breathing. Wendy always burrowed when she lapsed into a deep sleep.

Pamela went into the bathroom as he undressed and climbed thankfully into bed, leaving his clothes in a pile on the floor. He was already drifting off when he felt her slide in beside him. Her arms encircled his shoulders and she rested her head on his chest. He tried to speak to her, but the black abyss opened and sleep greedily reached out to claim him for its own.

******

PART TWO

THE NIGHTMARES BEGIN

CHAPTER FOUR

THE WHITE ROOM

The room was of an intense white, which appeared to give off its own light and impart to all its fittings and occupants a hazy quality. He was acutely aware of his own nakedness. Pamela and Wendy were also there, both naked and helpless between indistinct figures leading them away from him. He tried to follow, but it was as if every painful movement had to be forced from unresponsive muscles. Then he was on a table, pinned to its cold, smooth surface by a blinding white light which seemed to penetrate his entire being. Indistinct faces stared down at him as he lay helpless and he could almost smell his own fear. One being reached a spindly hand out to him and covered his face.

The brilliant whiteness faded and the image transformed itself into the familiar surroundings of their bedroom. The bed was damp around his head and he was sweating profusely. He slowly swung his body round and sat on the edge of the bed for a moment before he ran clammy hands through his tousled hair and stood up. He groped along the wall for the bathroom light switch and snapped it on. He headed for the sink and rinsed his face with cold water until the sweating subsided. He turned off the noisy flow of water and reached for a towel. He began to dab his face dry when a strange noise pierced the silence of the house. He stiffened in horror when he realised that it was coming from their bedroom.

He dropped the towel and raced into the bedroom. Pamela was sitting upright in bed, clawing at the bedclothes and screaming hysterically, wild eyes starting out of her sweat-drenched face. Her screaming reached a crescendo as events in her nightmare took a new turn.

“LEAVE HER ALONE YOU BASTARDS!! LEAVE MY DAUGHTER ALONE. WENDY!! LEAVE HER ALONE. I’LL KILL YOU!! YOU BASTARDS!!”

Alan shook her and shouted her name until her eyes cleared and focussed on him. Immediately, she slumped into his arms and began to cry. He held her tightly as sobs wracked her shivering body. A movement at the doorway caught his attention. Wendy stood there, rubbing sleep clouded eyes and squinting in the light.

"What is it, love?"

"I've been having a bad dream. What's wrong with mum?"

"Nothing, she'll be okay in a few minutes. Now go back to bed."

"I can't find my way; the bulb's gone in my room."

Alan relented and allowed her to sit on the corner of the bed as he attempted to calm Pamela down. He couldn't send the child back to her bedroom alone if her dream had been anything like his. Pamela's sobs gradually subsided and she lay back, exhausted. Alan stood up and turned to Wendy.

"Come on, you, it's time for you to get back to bed."

"What about the light in my bedroom?"

"I'll fix it right now. Come on."

He rummaged through various cupboards until he found a light bulb. He inserted it into the fitting in Wendy's room and switched it on to assure her that it was, indeed, functional. She climbed back into bed and allowed him to tuck her in,

something which he had not done for years. He wiped her hair gently away from her forehead and bent to kiss her softly.

"It was just a bad dream love, now go back to sleep."

She smiled, but it was a thin disguise behind which hid childish night-time fears and worries. He kissed her softly again before tousling her hair.

"Come on, the bogeyman can't get at you in here."

He turned to switch off the light, but Wendy reached out a pleading hand.

"No, leave the light on, dad."

He smiled comfortingly.

"Okay. No wonder your bulbs don't last two minutes!"

He left the room and closed the door softly before returning to his bedroom. Pamela was still sitting up in bed and nervously lighting a cigarette with shaking fingers. He saw that the packet was an ancient one which she had kept after giving up smoking five years ago. The unfamiliar curl of blue smoke which drifted towards the ceiling brought home to him the effect which the dream had on Pamela. He sat down beside her and put a comforting arm around her shoulder.

"What the hell's going on, Pamela?"

She coughed on the cigarette and spoke in a dry voice.

"I don't know but there has to be an explanation for all of this."

Alan was not convinced, but he knew that the time was not right for him to voice his fears.

"Perhaps you're right."

He glanced at the bedside digital clock which read 03:54. He was tired and irritable and he knew that any discussion begun now would soon degenerate into the now-familiar argument. He climbed back into bed, Pamela finished the cigarette. She held the filter tip between index finger and thumb and grimaced.

"That's the last time I touch one of those damned things for a long time."

Alan looked down at her.

"You look like you needed that."

"You're telling me I did. I don't know what the hell's happening with her tonight."

He held her closer.

"Don't worry about it; we can talk in the morning."

She shifted down in the bed and settled onto her pillows.

"Damned right we can, I'm buggered."

Alan settled down beside her and they moved as close as possible to each other. He kissed her neck gently.

"Me too."

He snapped the light off and closed his eyes. Immediately the images flooded back and his eyelids snapped open almost involuntary. He could hear and feel Pamela's steady breathing, but he knew that peaceful sleep was evading her as well. He watched the figures on the clock slowly count time until a dim grey prelude to the rapidly-approaching day began to seep through the curtains.

He rose and threw them back, staring out into the barely-lit world. With each dawn a magic hung in the air and he could see it gathering in the rugged hills to the east. The breaking day began to colour his dreams with objectivity and his fear gradually dissolved. Why have such a strange dream? He searched through his memories of the past few months for any disturbing books or films which he may have seen, but this proved useless. He secretly knew that he had never seen anything which could have conjured up the bizarre and hazy dreamscape which had disturbed him so much. He looked across at Pamela's sleeping form and narrowed his eyes as he noticed the faintest of quivers in her muscles which indicated a light and dream-filled sleep. As he watched, her eyes snapped open and she left the bed almost immediately, rubbing her sleep-clouded eyes and scrutinising the clock.

"Five thirty-five! On a Saturday. This is getting ridiculous. Did you sleep?"

He shook his head.

"No, did you?"

She stood up and turned to face the mirror mounted on the wardrobe door.

"Does it look like it?"

He joined her and closely studied both reflections. The mirror showed two grey and weary people, one unshaven and both with black blotches under sleep-clouded eyes.

He left the room and locked himself in the bathroom where he stood under the shower for an hour and attempted to piece together the events of the last twenty hours. After towelling himself dry, he shaved and dressed. The rich smells of breakfast drifted through the closed door, but they did not set his mouth watering as they usually would have done. He descended the stairs quietly so as not to wake Wendy and cut through the living room into the kitchen.

Kissing Pamela on the head, he stepped out into the cool morning and took deep breaths of the biting air. He noticed that he had not put the car away last night and he inspected its shiny bodywork closely for any damage which he might have missed during last night's inspection.

His search was, once again, fruitless. Pamela's voice announcing breakfast sailed through the open door. He worked his way through the meal without enthusiasm and appetite and they both left a considerable amount of food on their plates. Pamela left the table without a word and reappeared in the same silent manner half an hour later, showered and fully dressed.

The same silence prevailed throughout the post breakfast chores of tidying and washing up and seemed to suffocate Alan as they both performed unnecessary menial tasks in order to keep their minds occupied. Alan's attention was drawn by cries from the cul-de-sac.

The children from the house two doors down were beginning a rowdy early morning game of football. Early risers were beginning to show themselves armed with lawnmowers and car shampoo. The noise of traffic from the road which ran along the valley bottom below the estate began to grow and he felt that the world was beginning to awaken. With this awakening came a change of mood and a lifting of spirits.

He was once again sure that there had to be some explanation for last night's strange events. He seriously considered the possibility that they had left the play later than they had thought and then spent longer than expected at Pamela's parents' house. He headed for the telephone, intending to confirm this by ringing Brian.

Brian's voice sounded slurred and dry. Alan realised that he had most probably got him out of bed.

"Hi? Brian? Yeah, it's Alan here. This may seem a bit daft coming from me, but what time did we leave the play last night?"

"What time did who leave the play?"

"Us, me and Wendy."

"Huh? Why ask? What's up, Alan?"

"Nothing's up. Just tell me."

Brian raised his voice in question.

"About eight thirty? What is this Alan, you in trouble with Pamela?"

"Sort of."

"You want to talk? We can meet somewhere if you want."

This was the last thing he wanted right now. He tried to kick his sluggish mind into finding a way of terminating the conversation without being short and without worrying Brian. He could find none.

"Er, well, I've got a lot on today. Look, I'll see you Monday."

"Yeah, okay, Al, but maybe we should talk before then?"

"You're okay. Maybe I'll see you in the pub tomorrow."

"Sure."

"Okay, bye."

He replaced the receiver without waiting for a reply. Growing confusion began to contort his rational train of thought and he found images of his nightmare once again flooding into his brain. He snatched the receiver from its cradle once more and began to dial Albert and Margaret Kelly's number. The phone was answered almost immediately and he heard Albert's deep and well modulated voice announce the number. He steadied with a single breath.

"Albert? Hi, it's Alan. I'm just ringing to thank you for your hospitality last night."

"That's okay, Alan. Did you and Pamela have a good meal last night?"

A hundred possible answers flooded into Alan's head, but he felt almost compelled to tell Albert the truth. This fought an equally powerful compulsion to deny that there was any component of reality within last night's strange events. He must have been silently grappling with this for some time because Albert's voice made him start.

"Are you still there, Alan?"

"Er, yeah. I'm just not awake yet. Did you manage to record the snooker match?"

"Yes, I did. You can drop by today and pick it up if you want. That way there's less chance of you overhearing the result."

"I completely forgot about it myself. We got a bit delayed on the way home and I was too tired to do anything other than sleep last night what with the play and everything. Just out of interest, what time did we leave last night anyway?"

Albert's surprisingly prompt answer was mixed with an undertone of curiosity.

"Around nine thirty, I'm not too sure of the exact time. How did you get delayed? That car of yours shouldn't have broken down."

"We got stuck in a bit of mist on the way home and I think I hit an animal, though there's no damage to the car."

"That's not unusual in these parts, Alan, neither is the lack of damage to your car. Can't say I saw any mist myself last night."

"It was an isolated patch; we were no sooner in it than it had cleared."

"Hmm, well, if you hit an animal, you'd be best reporting it to the police. That's somebody's livelihood we're talking about, you know."

"Yeah, I already have done. They say they'll get in touch with me if they have to."

"You should be okay, then. Just give your car a thorough check before going out in it again, though."

"Will do, Albert, thanks for the advice. I'll try and get over today if I get the time."

Alan was already replacing the receiver as Albert was saying his goodbyes. He stood for a while in deep thought before dialling the number of the local police station. He recognised the voice of the officer to which Wendy had spoken last night and was glad that he had caught him before his shift ended.

"This is Mr. Morrison here. I believe my wife rang last night regarding a possible collision with an animal. I was wondering if you'd had any reports of injured animals from the local farmers."

The policeman muttered 'animals' to himself as he leafed through his notes. Alan heard him move the phone to prop his pad open at the relevant page.

"Yes, sir. No, we've had no reports of injured animals in the area. Is there any damage to your vehicle?"

"I haven't had a good look, but there doesn't appear to be any at all.

"I see. Well, I'll take your details, if I may, and I'll ask around among the farmers to see if there have been any of their animals straying onto the road."

Alan reeled off his details, thanked the policeman and rang off. After another pause for thought, he rang the number of the local paper. He spoke to Andrew Howarth, the paper's assistant editor and local reporter who was only moderately interested in his story of straying sheep. After Alan had stressed the dangers of stray animals being present on the area's unlit roads, he grudgingly promised that he would personally write a short piece asking farmers and motorists alike to remain vigilant.

For the rest of the morning, he and Pamela continued with more tasks and deliberately avoided speaking of their nightmares.

Wendy rose unusually late and seemed subdued and listless. Alan persuaded her to help him wash the car, but he noticed that she spent more time staring absentmindedly at the dripping sponge which she held in her hand rather than anything else. He worked diligently, absorbed in the task of inspecting the vehicle for any damage, even slight, which could explain the bump which they felt last night upon leaving the mist. He waxed every inch of the vehicle's paintwork and failed to find a scratch. His inspection of the under body revealed no breaches to the sealant and no sign whatsoever of an impact. He was sure that if they had hit something at least some marks would have been left, even if the vehicle itself wasn't damaged to any great extent. He ended his search with some degree of bemusement and went back into the house. Wendy and Pamela were both shrugging on light summer jackets and preparing to leave as he entered the living room. Pamela anticipated his question.

"We're going into town. Do you want anything?"

"No, I'm fine. Do you want a lift?"

Pamela shook her head.

"We'll get the bus."

He gave her a shrug of indifferent agreement and escorted them both to the door. Wendy said a half-hearted goodbye to him before they walked down the drive and across the cul-de-sac to a small path which crossed the fields behind the house and joined the main road.

With them gone, the house felt strangely silent and cold despite the unseasonable heat of the autumn sun. For the first time since last night, he switched on the television. He was half hoping that there had been problems with all of the clocks last night, that it really was around 10pm when they arrived home and that the TV had just been malfunctioning. His hopes faded as the screen brightened and the imaged resolved itself into that of a woman reading the late morning news. He flicked idly through the channels and encountered perfect reception on them all.

He finally flicked back to the channel which was broadcasting a cartoon and tried to let the slapstick antics of the characters amuse him. He found, however, that he couldn't absorb even something that simple and instead rose and pulled the TV's plug from its socket. Before straightening up, he once again checked the video clock against the one on the mantelpiece and then compared them both with his own wristwatch. They all agreed on a time of eleven twenty. He slipped into the kitchen and checked the wall clock in the hope that some anomaly may turn up. This, too, was in stubborn agreement with the rest. He looked round the kitchen for a moment before his eyes settled on his car keys. He snatched them up impulsively and left the house.

As he headed back towards the village, he found that the car was lacking power even when driven hard, a time when it used to excel. As it laboured away from the junction beyond The Rope and Anchor, he made a mental note to have a word with Philip Bellamy, the proprietor of the local garage.

As he passed the garage, he slowed down and looked into its gloomy interior in search of the mechanic. The building appeared deserted and the distinctive shape of Bellamy's Triumph was nowhere to be seen. He pulled off the main road and joined the familiar route leading to his school. Once there, he pulled into the deserted car park and paused to set the timer function of his wristwatch before restarting the engine and heading back towards the village. He followed the road through the fork beyond the pub and headed up the side of the hill towards Pamela's parents' house.

Twice the car stalled as he followed the narrow, curving road and the second time he encountered severe difficulty when he tried to restart the engine. He finally reached the point where the road narrowed and turned to run in front of the small row of terraced houses, ending at a gate just beyond the last house where Albert and Margaret Kelly lived.

He turned the car and drove back down the hill, rejoining the main road and following it at a steady speed until he reached the turn-off leading to their cul-de-sac. He stopped at the end of their drive and glanced at his watch. The timer showed that the entire journey had taken just over sixty minutes.

He paused for a while, feeling helpless and confused as he went through possible explanations again and again in his tired mind. None fitted the obvious facts nor did they explain the strange events of their journey. His mind drifted slowly back to the unlit road and the wall of green mist. He thoughtfully turned the car round and headed back towards the village.

He found a convenient lay-by adjacent to the spot where they had first encountered the mist and parked the car before walking along the area of road which it had engulfed. He found no evidence of a collision of any sort, but still considered the possibility that whatever they had hit had managed to crawl the short distance to the fields beyond the high roadside wall.

He crossed the road and miscalculated his vault of the gate, landing heavily and twisting his ankle. The fall had knocked the breath from him and he lay for a moment before tentatively flexing his bruised limb. He grimaced at the pain and slowly began to get to his feet.

A shadow loomed above him and blocked out the sun for a moment. He found himself staring into the broad smiling face of Philip Bellamy. He was a ridiculously tall, slightly-built man with piercing blue eyes and a slim, smiling face which was partially obscured at times by an uncontrollable mass of curly blonde hair. He was rarely seen in anything other than blue overalls and those he wore were frayed and greasy. He had obviously left the garage in a hurry. Alan allowed himself to be hauled to his feet and planted back on the ground. Philip's smile broadened.

"You want to take things a bit easier, Al; you're getting a bit too old for this kind of thing."

Alan laughed for a moment before following Philip's gaze as he turned away and began casting around the ground surface near to the gate, once more absorbed in what he had been doing before Alan had arrived.

"Have you lost anything, Phil?"

He stood up and wiped his dusty hands on his overalls, replacing the dry soil with dirty engine grease.

"No, but I am looking for something."

"What do you mean?"

Philip looked at him, surprise showing on his bright face.

"Haven't you heard? A few people have reported seeing a UFO round here last night."

Alan did not make the connection for a moment, until he remembered Philip's interest in the subject. Despite his tiredness and confusion, he smiled to himself. He knew of nobody except Philip who would spend their Saturday mornings searching a fallow field for evidence of a UFO landing. Philip cast one final glance around the area before turning back to Alan.

"Anyway, what can I do for you, Al?"

Alan remembered the reason for his impulsive journey.

"We were coming home last night and we ran into some fog. I think we hit a sheep or something and I was wondering whether it managed to get back into the field before it died. There's nothing on the road."

Philip laughed for a moment.

"Aye, and no sheep along this area of the road. You sure it wasn't a cow? There was something in the paper about them this morning."

Alan recalled his request to Andrew Howarth and was pleased that the popular reporter had taken the time to honour it so soon before the paper began its small print run.

"I rang the local paper because I thought that something had got out of the fields onto the road last night. We were lucky I guess because we had to slow down once we got into the fog. It could have been a lot worse otherwise."

Philip nodded and pursed his lips in thought.

"I've had a look round the fields either side of this stretch of road and I haven't seen anything. You sure it wasn't a rock off one of the walls?"

Alan shook his head.

"No way. Something like that would have made a hell of a mess of the car, but I can't find a scratch. Speaking of problems though, it is feeling a bit sluggish. You know, not quite its usual self."

The mention of a malfunctioning car caught and held Philip's attention.

"Sluggish in what way? Brakes binding?"

"No, the engine just seems to be lacking power. I didn't notice it until just now."

Philip turned and headed back towards the road.

"Crack the lid and I'll have a look now if you want. Could be something simple."

Alan opened the bonnet and revealed what seemed to him to be little more than a tangled mess of pipes, wires of varying thickness and protruding sections of metal. Philip leaned over the engine until his hair brushed its surface and thrust his arms deep into its interior. After a few moments of experimental tugging and twisting, he straightened up and gestured to the driver's seat.

"Try it now."

Alan twisted the key and the engine stuttered into life reluctantly. It idled roughly for a short moment before cutting out once more. Philip shook his head.

"That is sick. You'd better bring it in as soon as possible."

Alan got out of the car and looked under the bonnet himself in search of inspiration.

"Yeah, it's got worse. What do you think it is?"

Philip tugged and twisted for another short moment and then straightened up again.

"Looks a bit like the fuel injection are shot. Bit weird for these things though, it should last forever."

"What's that going to cost?"

The mechanic gazed at the sky and made a sharp upward gesture with his thumb. Alan slumped back against the car's wing.

"Somehow I knew you were going to say that."

"Sorry, mate. That's German engineering for you."

He glanced at his watch and seemed surprised by the time.

"Christ! I've got to be getting back. I'm expecting a call at twelve-thirty. See you later, Al, and don't forget to run that in for me to have a look at it. Don't drive any further than you have to till then."

He walked over to his Triumph which he had parked behind the hedge beyond the road. Alan coaxed the Passat into life and pulled onto the road. In a matter of moments, he heard a harsh snarling which increased in pitch and volume as Bellamy caught him. He flashed his lights once, blipped the car's throttle and overtook him in a flash. On a good day, Alan would have given him a race back to the village. His prime concern now was nursing the car at any speed and he held this in mind as he slowly turned round and headed back home.

He was greeted by a shrill cry of childish excitement as he walked slowly up the drive. Wendy ran out holding a poster and proudly showed Alan the glossy picture of her blue-eyed, blonde-haired teenage idol.

"Dad! Can I stick Jason up in my room? Mom says I have to ask you."

He nodded.

"Okay, but use Blu-tak. No Sellotape and NO drawing pins."

"Thanks, dad."

She giggled for a moment before turning round and running back into the house. Alan followed her and was greeted by the deliciously savoury smell of cooking. He kissed Pamela on the top of her head as he walked into the kitchen.

"Smells great, what is it?"

"Nothing special, just spaghetti bolognaises."

She continued to stir the sauce for a moment before turning the heat down under the pan and propping the spoon against the back of the cooker. She turned to Alan and slipped her arms round his waist.

"Where have you been until this time?"

"Just driving, and thinking."

She leant her head on one side and smiled coyly.

"Oh? What about?"

Alan became irritated by her flippant attitude.

"You know damn well what about."

She withdrew her arms and walked over to the sink. When she spoke again her voice was no longer soft, but insistent and edgy.

"Alan, I wish you wouldn't talk about that. I'd rather forget it."

He walked over to join her.

"Oh yeah, forget a couple of hours which we can't account for? Forget the dreams? Forget that it all happened?"

The tense silence was interrupted by a bubbling noise from the cooker. The lid on the pan of spaghetti was being slowly pushed up by a white mass of foam. As they both watched, the pan boiled over and the liquid sizzled as it hit the hot metal of the hob. Pamela shouted in exasperation and moved to lift the pan off the stove. Alan tried to sidestep her and do the same, but he stumbled, causing her to knock against the handle and spill its contents onto the cooker and surrounding work surfaces. She spun round.

"Now look what you've done! Are you happy now? Just get lost for a bit and let me sort this mess out!"

He opened his mouth to say something, but the words left his mind and dried in the back of his throat. He turned on his heel and went into the living room, slumping down in an armchair and gazing at the paper.

Pamela finished preparing the meal and it was eaten in a silence that was only occasionally broken by Wendy as she enthusiastically began a conversation which her parents refused to be drawn into.

Eventually, her chatter subsided and she cleared her plate, refusing a second course. She switched on the TV and was soon giggling at a Saturday afternoon cartoon show. Alan and Pamela carried their tense silence on through the washing up and well into the evening, both feigning interest in the repeat of an ancient war movie. Pamela became aware of a rapidly increasing weight against her arm. She looked down at Wendy who was fast asleep against her and then at Alan who nodded.

"Yeah, I'll take her up."

Pamela gently nudged her awake and Wendy took the hand which Alan held out to her. He glanced at his watch as he led her up the stairs and was surprised to find that it read just after 9pm. He thought back a few years and realised that Wendy hadn't been to bed this early on a Saturday since the age of nine. He tried not to let his concern show as he tucked her in at her request, but he asked her if she was feeling well. She managed a wan smile.

"Yeah, I'm just tired, dad."

He smiled back and ruffled her hair before kissing her forehead gently.

"Okay love, you go to sleep now."

He straightened up and opened the door. As he reached to switch off the light, she called to him from under the covers.

"No, dad, leave the light on for a bit please."

He didn't argue, but her request served only to deepen his concern. He was sure that there was more than a trace of pleading in her voice, which suddenly sounded more like that of a frightened child's. He descended the stairs quietly and found that the television was off and that Pamela was also slipping into a light sleep on the couch. His voice awoke her as he began to speak.

"I'll open the bottle of wine if you want."

Pamela rose, unsteady from her few moments of sleep, and headed for the cabinet holding the glasses. Alan pulled the bottle from the fridge and began to struggle with the cork. As he did this, he broke the silence which had once more settled.

"I followed the route which we took last night again today. It only took me sixty minutes, so that still leaves us without an explanation for at least three hours. I also met Philip Bellamy on the way back. You know he's into UFOs and little green men?"

Pamela nodded.

"Well, didn't Wendy see a shooting star last night?"

Pamela walked through into the kitchen and set the glasses down on the worktop. She turned to Alan and he saw that her tired face bore a worried expression.

"What are you trying to say, Alan?"

He reached the end of his line of reasoning almost thankfully when he saw the effect it was having upon her.

"Nothing, I just wondered if perhaps that shooting star had been the UFO that some people reported to Philip."

Her quick nod appeared to dismiss the whole question of UFOs in an instant. She gestured to the now open wine bottle.

"Are we going to have that before it starts to taste like old dishwater?"

Alan filled both their glasses which they took back into the living room along with the bottle. They drank in silence for a while before Pamela set down her glass and moved forward in the seat to rest her elbows on her knees.

"I think that whatever happened on Friday night was just a fluke. You know, one of those things which just occur once without explanation? We may have got lost and taken a long time to get home without even realising it. You know yourself that one bit of road can start to look like another in the dark. I've known the time myself when I can't remember whole sections of a journey, even though I must have passed through familiar areas."

Alan didn't know whether it was wine, his tiredness or a combination of the two, but Pamela's explanation for the missing time was compelling. It would be so easy to take a wrong turn in the dark and it could be possible that time spent following back roads could be forgotten once he rejoined the main highway and continued along their usual route home. He tried to remember whether the car had consumed as excessive amount of petrol on the way home on Friday. He couldn't recall noticing anything strange today, but was aware that the car's faulty electrical system could be causing instrumentation error as well. It all seemed to make sense. Pamela could see acceptance in his face and she continued to press her point with determination.

"It could be that we passed through an area with no landmarks so there wouldn't be anything to remember. Whatever went on I think we should forget it. There's no harm done. We can start to worry if it happens again."

Alan thankfully agreed with her and sat back with an almost tangible sense of relief. He felt the tension of the last thirty hours begin to slide from his body to be

replaced with a gorgeously warm and satisfyingly numbing sense of tiredness. He poured himself another glass of wine and emptied the remains into Pamela's half-empty glass. They toasted each other silently and felt the wine warm them from within.

Alan's tiredness began to drag at his eyelids and he stood up, fighting to retain his balance as the wine began to take effect. Pamela stood and plunged the room into darkness as she switched off the lights. They climbed the stairs by the orange glow of the streetlamp outside which filtered through the net curtains dimly. Pamela began to undress as Alan headed for the bathroom.

After a half-hearted attempt to brush his teeth, he slid into bed and propped himself up on one arm to watch Pamela as she undressed. He allowed his eyes to play over the smooth curves of her body and he felt himself aroused despite his tiredness. She turned and his eyes settled on a small red mark just above her navel. He pointed to it and Pamela looked down, suddenly reddening with unexplainable self-consciousness.

"What's that? I've not noticed it before."

She touched the mark lightly and shook her head before slipping on her nightdress.

"I don't know. It just appeared this morning. It doesn't hurt at all, so I've not worried about it."

She slipped into bed and they moved into each other's welcoming embrace. Pamela wedged her head comfortably into the crook of his arm. She laughed softly for a moment and stared reflectively at the ceiling. Alan turned to her.

"What?"

"Nothing. I was just thinking what I could do to you if I wasn't so knackered."

He smiled ruefully.

"Yeah. Maybe tomorrow, eh?"

He shivered a little as her hand drifted onto his stomach. She closed her eyes.
"Turn off the light will you, Alan? My head feels like it's going to explode."

He reached out and fumbled for a moment before finding the switch. He brought the day to an end with a decisive click and closed his eyes, feeling a moment's worry pass as he remembered the small red mark which he had found behind his ear that morning as he had shaved.

******

CHAPTER FIVE

THE SHARED DREAM

The mist moved in closer against the windows of the car until it seemed as if it was a glutinous animal which threatened to break through the glass and smother them all. A shape appeared at the back window and, when it moved, Alan could see that it was a large head, hairless, with shining, black, cat-like eyes. Wendy saw it out of the corner of her eye, screaming with fright as she turned to look straight at it. The mist in front of them was suddenly lit from within by an eerie, pulsing glow. The light brightened and the mist slowly parted.

Alan stared, aghast, at the huge, dome-shaped object which straddled the road ahead of them, blocking any route of escape. A white ramp led up to an opening high in the upper dome, from which emanated an intense, white light. Other faces began to appear at the car windows as the mist lost some of its cohesiveness and began to drift away. He looked across at Pamela, whose head lolled against the seat in her fear-induced blackout. A sickening dizziness swept through him for a moment and he fought to retain his own consciousness. He gripped the steering wheel of the car and blinked fiercely.

Spinning shapes and dancing colours finally resolved themselves into a large circular room. Five small beings moved to the car and Alan found himself leaving its protective security and stepping out into the room. He felt a pang of fear as he saw that Wendy and Pamela were also opening doors and leaving their seats. One of the creatures moved to face him and he realised how small they were. In a flash of fear-borne irrationality he remembered the first year class he had taught that day and realised that these things were even shorter than the children, perhaps only four and a half feet tall. Their grotesquely bulbous heads seemed to be entirely hairless and held no recognisable features with the exception of their huge eyes, which seemed to penetrate into his very being. Their spindly bodies were covered by loose-fitting garments, which fastened just below their pointed chins. Their skin was a sickly grey colour and appeared to be parchment-thin.

Two others moved forward and slipped their thin hands into his. He felt a revulsion bordering on nausea, but this passed in a moment and was replaced by a deep feeling of calmness and contentment as he allowed himself to be led from the circular chamber into a smaller ante-room. In his bliss, he looked round for Wendy and Pamela and could see no sign of them. He felt as if he should go and look for them, but there was another flash of light.

He instead found himself pinned to a bare white table. He was powerless to move and he could only look on helplessly as the beings moved towards his now-naked body. One took hold of his limp penis as the other one produced a long shining instrument and quickly thrust it into his helpless organ. The pain grated at his brain and he let out a scream which clawed at the back of his throat. One of the two performing the bizarre examination passed a hand over his face impassively and the pain faded instantly. Voices welled up from the depths of his subconscious mind, all united in their chorus of reassurance.

The light above the table flared into a brightness which forced him to close his eyes. When he opened them again, he found himself standing next to Pamela and Wendy, both of whom were also naked. The family embraced each other and then found their attention directed to a panel on the far wall of the room which sprang into life as they looked at it.

They glimpsed their own planet hanging in a sea of blackness for a moment before the image was replaced by rapidly alternating scenes of shattered war fields, famine-ridden deserts, rusting chemical dumps, decaying cities and rotting forests. With each new scene, they were met by a profound sense of loss, deafened by the cries of fear and anguish, and numbed as they felt the pain of billions. The flashing images reached a crescendo of colour and suddenly ceased.

They were surprised for a moment by the silence and they allowed themselves to be led submissively into the circular room where the car awaited them. Alan turned to look at Pamela and realised that they were all fully clothed again. They climbed back into the car and the beings once again clustered around them. He thought he recognised the one which had first looked up at him, which now stood in front of the car.

He looked for a moment at the shining eyes and felt they conveyed a message. Despite everything, he smiled at the creature and, at that moment, there seemed to be a brief, yet direct, link between them. The being returned his smile and his expression conveyed remarkable benevolence. The mist began to close in again and the creatures were suddenly gone from view. It was as if they had left a fantasy and returned to reality. Pamela's last word hung in the air as they all felt a sharp bump. He recognised the familiar road which wound away from them into the night.

He was met by the same darkness as his eyelids snapped open. The merest trace of insanity clouded his eyes for an instant before he sat up in bed like a grotesque manikin having its strings tightened by a cruel puppet master. His hand shot to the light switch and he blinked at its brightness as he switched it on. Beside him, Pamela tossed her head in an uneasy sleep. He shook her sharply and her eyes stared at him blankly for a moment as she woke before she also sat up and began to cry uncontrollably.

Alan didn't even bother to ask her what her dream was about. They both rose shakily and dressed, feeling that their sleep had actually sapped them of energy rather than replacing that which they had lost the day before.

As the sun rose, he quietly opened Wendy's door and drew some comfort from the fact that she was sleeping peacefully. He descended the stairs and quietly walked through the kitchen. Pamela was pouring boiling water into mugs which they both huddled around as they sat at the kitchen table. Pamela sniffed back tears as she took a sip of the steaming liquid. She spoke in a cracked, weak voice.

"We've got to tell someone about this, Alan."

He nodded.

"I know, but who?"

Pamela put down her mug almost as if the weight had been too much for her. Alan noticed that her shoulders sagged and that she looked drawn and tired. He felt little different. Now she spoke slowly, with many pauses for consideration, groping for order among the chaos.

"We saw a shooting star on Friday night. Then we drove into that mist. Now we're having these dreams and everything is going crazy. I'm not saying there's a link, but don't you think that there might be something in the mist which made us dream these things after seeing the star?"

Alan forced his unwilling mind to act. He remembered what Philip Bellamy had said about UFOs. A week ago, he would have dismissed the thought immediately.

He now left the table and reached for the telephone book. He found Bellamy's number listed under the name of his garage and he was about to begin dialling when he glanced at his watch. It read 6:30am, too early to call. He slowly put the receiver back into its cradle and made a note of the number. He went back to the table and finished his mug of tea. Pamela pushed her mug away.

"I don't think we should say anything to Wendy about this."

Alan remembered Wendy's frightened face with a clarity which should not have been held within a mere dream. He could hardly bring himself to think of the damage which this experience could have done to her if any component of reality had been present within it. He was thankful that she didn't appear to have had any more dreams after the nightmare of Friday night.

"Okay. We won't say a word to her unless she starts having the same dreams. Then we'll have to tell her."

Pamela nodded in agreement.

"We'll worry about that if it starts to happen, Alan."

He took the tea mug away from her and went to the sink, where he began to wash them. They busied themselves with the task of making an early breakfast and they ate it slowly as the clock's hands crept along their lonely journey around its numbered face.

Alan left at 8am to buy the Sunday newspaper and he headed for the telephone as soon as he arrived home some thirty minutes later. He hoped that Philip Bellamy was not getting out of bed to answer the phone as he heard it connect and began to ring. He was relieved when Bellamy's voice answered and announced the name of the garage. Alan wondered if he ever stopped working.

"Philip? It's Alan Morrison here. I wondered if I could have a word with you at some point today?"

Philip was as bright and cheerful as always. Alan wondered how long the mood would last once he had told him his story.

"Yeah, sure. If it's about your car, then it's good news. I don't think the repairs will cost anything like what I thought they might do."

"Er, yeah, thanks. No, it's not really about the car. I'd just like to talk to you."

Philip seemed undaunted by the strange request. "Sure. What's all this about, Alan? Something wrong?"

Alan saw no point in disguising anything, but he felt he couldn't tell Philip everything over the telephone.

"Yeah, you could say that."

"Okay, look. I've got to finish up here, but I can be over at your place by eleven. How does that sound?"

Alan was surprised by the mechanic's promptness, but he found it reassuring. He nodded to Pamela before voicing his agreement. Philip rang off almost immediately after the arrangements had been confirmed.

Though neither would admit it, they were both relieved that Philip would be arriving in a matter of hours. Pamela was about to say something when Wendy sailed into the kitchen with a bright 'good morning' and immediately began to prepare herself a huge bowl of breakfast cereal. In that respect, she was the same as Pamela, possessing the capability to happily eat large meals without putting on an ounce in weight. Alan looked pointedly at Pamela and she smiled. They were both relieved that these strange events appeared not to have affected their daughter in any way. Wendy began to eat her breakfast and spoke between mouthfuls.

"What are we going to do today, dad?"

Alan thought of Philip's impending arrival and suddenly realised that she would hear everything if she was present at the meeting. He was conscious of the time and frantically began to think of a place where she could go for a few hours and would not appear to her to be too out of the ordinary.

"I don't have any plans really. What do you think?"

"I was wondering if I could go over to Julie's for a bit. I think she's going to the cinema with her mum and dad."

He tried to look as if he was considering her request as normal, but something in his unusually quick response made Wendy look up from the table and gaze at him for a moment.

"You sure it's okay, dad? You didn't have anything else planned did you?"

"No, I just don't feel like doing much today and I don't want you to have to mope around with me all day. Do you want to give Julie a ring?"

Wendy shook her head.

"No, she'll ring me later and we'll sort it out then. Can I go over there for lunch?

This time his response seemed less hurried and Wendy's uneasiness seemed to disappear.

"As long as you aren't making a nuisance of yourself."

Wendy giggled.

"Julie's mum always makes too much for them to eat. I think I'll be doing her a favour."

"Okay, do you want me to take you over there?"

"No, I'll walk. It's not far."

Alan smiled at Pamela as she leant against the doorframe.

As Wendy predicted, Julie phoned an hour or so later and the friends made their arrangements and she left just before eleven. The roar of Philip's Triumph reverberated around the crescent just after 11am. He pulled into their driveway and parked neatly behind Alan's Passat. Alan met him as he got out of the car and he was surprised to see that the mechanic was dressed respectably and was carrying a miniature tape recorder which was balanced atop pile of files and a large notebook. Alan led him into the living room, where Pamela greeted him warmly and not without a degree of relief at his arrival. Alan was surprised to see that Philip seemed prepared and undaunted. He gratefully accepted a hot cup of coffee before shuffling his papers and set up his tape recorder on the coffee table. Alan sat back in his seat and silence fell upon the room until Philip spoke.

"I hope you don't mind me jumping to a few conclusions. I guessed this had to be something to do with the UFO sighting which you spoke to me about yesterday, Alan. Am I right?"

Alan nodded in agreement.

"Yeah. Sort of anyway."

Philip engaged the ball of his pen with a sharp click and opened his notepad.

"Well, I've had a few reports from people describing lights in the sky in this area on Friday night and what I'm really trying to do is get an idea of what kind of area the sightings cover."

Pamela seemed genuinely interested in this.

"How long have you been doing this for?"

"I've been a member of the British UFO Investigations Bureau for about ten years, but I've been interested in this kind of thing since I was a young lad. What I'd like to do now is ask you a few questions and record what you say if you've no objections?"

Neither of them had any objections, though they were conscious of each other's nervousness as Philip switched his tape recorder on. He began by recording the date and time of the interview and then he asked them to give an account of their sighting. Alan was surprised by his attentiveness as he began to relate the events of Friday evening. He paused at a point in his recollection of the journey just before they sighted the mist. Philip looked up from his notepad, which he had scribbled on occasionally as he has listened.

"Is that where it ended, then?" asked Philip.

Alan shook his head.

"No, there's more."

Philip gestured to the tape recorder.

"Do you want me to switch this off?"

Pamela sat forward in her chair.

"No, you may want to record this bit."

He smiled brightly and shrugged his shoulders.

"Whatever you are comfortable with is fine by me. Just carry on when you're ready."

They both told him of the green mist, the missing hours and then the nightmares. Philip seemed undaunted by this, merely utilising the occasional pause in their narrative to ask a short question or to scribble on his pad. When they had finished recounting the events of the last two nights, he stopped the tape without a word. Before he spoke Philip, turned a page in one of his files and made a tick with his pen.

"Okay, I just want to ask you a few questions about your interest in UFOs and some circumstances leading up to this event. You don't have to answer any of them if you don't want to."

Philip restarted the tape recorder and addressed them both, questioning them about their interest in UFOs and the paranormal in general. Neither of them had any interest and both agreed that the nearest they had got to the subject was taking Wendy to see the movie *ET - The Extra-Terrestrial* when it was running at the local cinema. He then moved on to question them about their personal circumstances in the months leading up to the event. Alan turned in his chair and spoke before Pamela had a chance to answer.

"Look, what's all this got to do with what's going on now? You don't think we're going crazy or something do you? This isn't just a dream you know. Something's happening."

Philip's voice was steady and reassuring.

"I don't think either of you are going crazy. It just helps us to build up a better picture of the circumstances surrounding the event if we know how you were feeling prior to it. You don't have to answer the questions if you don't want to but I assure you that this interview will remain confidential."

Alan sat back again and nodded.

"Yeah. Okay. Sorry about that, but I still don't see how it all fits into this."

Philip flipped back through his notebook for a moment before looking up at them both.

"It may not, but there are some possibilities which we have to cover.

Pamela raised her hands.

"Don't worry about it, Alan. We've got to get all of this sorted and if this is what it takes, then we'll have to go along with it."

Philip pointed to his tape recorder, but she shook her head.

"No, you may as well have it all."

They took turns in describing the increasing strain which they had been under on a day to day basis for the past few months and Pamela spoke of the affect which this had had upon their relationship. Both seemed surprised at the magnitude of the problems which were becoming apparent. There was a pause which was broken by a click as the spool of the tape recorder ended. Philip saw them consciously relax as they perceived that the interview was over. He quickly scribbled another note before turning to Pamela as she spoke.

"I know this sounds a little strange to you but it's only as we see things. I'm not saying for a moment that these are little green men or that there was a link between the shooting star that we saw and our later experiences. It just all seems to fit together."

Alan nodded in silent agreement and smiled a little in Pamela's direction.

"I hope you don't think we're mad or anything."

Philip was reassuring in his reply.

"There are others who have reported experiences similar to what you have just told me. I don't think for a moment that they were cranks and neither are you."

At the mention of similar experiences, they both appeared interested. Pamela asked the question for both of them.

"What became of those other people? What kind of experiences did they have?"

Philip retracted the ball on his pen with a flick of his thumb.

"Every person deals with an experience like this in a different way. There are differences between each experience which is reported, but they all basically follow the same pattern that yours has taken. Until I've looked into your case a bit further, I'm afraid I can't give you any answers."

Almost with a sense of sadness, he watched feelings of uncertainty, doubt and fear cloud their eyes as they realised he did not possess the answers they required. After a lifetime of interest, research and investigation, he himself feared that he was not capable of giving them all the answers even after a full investigation. He ticked off another section on his interview checklist and spoke once again to them both.

"I do not doubt the credibility of either of you here, but what you've told me is very remarkable. I have heard it before, like I've said, but you may find that others won't take the view that I have. It's obviously up to you who you tell now, but I'm just warning you to be prepared for some ridicule if you start bandying the story about."

Alan shook his head.

"We've decided to keep it all quiet until we know what's going on. Wendy doesn't seem to have been affected by this to the degree that we have been, so we've decided not to say anything, even to her, unless she starts having the dreams as well."

Philip nodded approvingly.

"That's probably the best thing to do under the circumstances. I'll go home now and get in touch with some friends of mine who also have experience of dealing with these kinds of things and I promise I'll speak to you both again very soon."

A worried look crossed Pamela's face.

"Friends?"

Philip chastised himself mentally as he realised what that would sound like to someone without knowledge of the intricate workings of the UFO research community.

"Don't worry. They're not all scruffy garage mechanics. A couple of people in this area have been at this for longer than I have and they may be able to advise me on the best course of action to take. I assure you that you can trust me."

Pamela's next question was delivered with more than a degree of suspicion.

"What exactly do your friends do? You don't mean doctors or anything like that do you?"

Philip lowered his eyes.

"Yes, one of them is a psychologist. But you have to understand that he won't be treating you, it's not my field to decide whether you have a problem or not. His primary interest will be in the experiences which you have reported to me. What you've got to understand is that I haven't had any experience of investigating things like this personally, but I do know that there is the potential for big mistakes to be made here if the situation is not handled correctly.

Pamela was reassured by this, but still seemed ill at ease. Philip shut his briefcase with a snap and locked it tightly before rising. As he did this, there came the sound of the outside door opening and laughter flooded into the kitchen. Wendy bounced in through the door, followed at a discreet distance by her friend, Julie. Both children seemed rather taken aback by Philip's presence, but Wendy responded brightly to his greeting and smiled before turning to her father.

"Dad, can Julie and I go listen to some music upstairs for a bit?"

Alan smiled at his daughter.

"Okay, but not too loud."

He turned to Julie.

"Have you both had a good time?"

She nodded, managing a subdued smile, despite the presence of both her teacher and Philip.

"We have thanks, Mr. Morrison."

Wendy turned to her mother, who hadn't spoken at all yet.

"What's for lunch, mum? It is okay if Julie stays?"

She smiled weakly and managed a barely discernable nod. Wendy's expression altered momentarily with surprise as she noticed her mother's condition, but she was distracted still further as her father stood up and began to show Philip to the door. Pamela appeared to become aware of her daughter's expression and she managed to compose herself.

"Sorry, Wendy, what did you say?"

Wendy's voice was insistent, with a little worry rather than anything else.

"I asked you what was for lunch. Can Julie stay? What's the matter, mum, are you not feeling well?"

Pamela shook her head.

"I'm fine, just a bit tired. I don't know what's for lunch, but Julie is more than welcome to join us."

She smiled.

"Thanks, Mrs Morrison, but I don't think I'm going to have time. Me and my dad are going to the rugby this afternoon."

"Okay. Why don't you have a word with Alan? He'll drive you home."

She barely had time to respond before Wendy dragged her through the door and up the stairs to her bedroom.

Alan paused at the front gate as Philip unlocked the door of his car. He stared at the sky in thought and when he spoke, his voice was dismissive, but held a deeper underline of insecurity and doubt.

"I'll admit that this has worried me, but I'm surprised at the impact it has had on Pamela. I think that we should get all of this in context before we go any further. This is the 20th century we're talking about today, not some time in the Dark Ages when one man could rule a whole village with talk of this kind of thing. Things like this just don't happen outside of science fiction movies do they?"

Philip placed his briefcase on the car's passenger seat and turned back to Alan. Leaning on the open car door with a thoughtful look on his face, he spoke agonisingly slowly, as if each word was the product of an unfamiliar train of thought.

"What we're dealing with here is something very complex which I don't fully understand. I do know that things like this have gone on elsewhere, but I don't know enough to be able to discuss these cases. This is why I have to enlist the help of people more knowledgeable in this field. Don't worry about the fact that this guy's a psychologist. As I've already said, his interest is in your experience, not yourselves. I can believe that you're both going through a difficult time because of this, but try not to worry, I don't think for a moment that either of you are going crazy."

He paused briefly in consideration before continuing. This time he seemed less confused as if back on familiar ground.

"I do think that you should do your best to keep this quiet for a while. I don't find what you've told me out of the ordinary, but I think you know yourself that other people may not be as understanding. I'm not trying to frighten you at all, but you should be prepared for the inevitable ridicule that would follow should you talk about this out in the open."

Alan shook his head decisively.

"We've already agreed to keep it quiet, mainly for Wendy's sake. She doesn't seem to be affected by all of this to the same degree that we are and I'm just hoping it will stay that way."

Philip reaffirmed his approval for this as he got into his car. As he prepared to start the engine he looked through the windscreen at Alan's Volkswagen lying in the drive. He remembered the fault which Alan had described to him when they had met in the field yesterday. He made the connection with their account of events which was still fresh in his mind and he felt the mystery deepen for him as another piece of a disturbingly familiar jigsaw puzzle fell into place.

Alan leant against the gate as the Triumph roared to life. Philip opened his window and shouted over the noise of the car's engine.

"If you need anything, day or night, or if you just want to talk for a while, then just give me a call. You've got my number, haven't you?"

Philip waved a dismissive hand.

He reversed slowly down the drive and waited until he had reached the bottom of the cul-de-sac before heading off out of the estate.

Alan went back into the house and was ignored by Pamela, who was engrossed in lunch preparations. As he entered the living room and sat down, he heard a dull throbbing of music from Wendy's bedroom above. He drew comfort again from the apparent lack of effect which the events of the past few days had had on her.

******

CHAPTER SIX

I JUST HAVE TO TALK TO SOMEONE

Philip Bellamy paused only to check the integrity of the locks on his Triumph before he ascended the stairs to his flat. As soon as he was through the door, he lifted a pole from its holder in the hall and lowered a steel loft ladder from a hatch in the ceiling above his head. He climbed up into the loft and rummaged through neglected, but well organised, files for a moment before extracting the one he required. Inside the folder were details of a case which Dr. Clarke had worked on some time ago. More importantly, the psychologist's address and telephone number were also held on a card attached to the file. He flicked the light off as he descended from the loft and made his way into the kitchen. As he put the kettle on to boil, he lifted the telephone and dialled the psychologist's number. The connection was made and the phone was answered almost immediately, a well-spoken and precise-sounding male voice answered the phone.

"Dr. Clarke? My name is Philip Bellamy. I wonder if I might borrow a few moments of your time in the hope you might be able to help me."

The psychologist indicated a cautious agreement.

"I've just spoken to a couple who are friends of mine. They are reporting a number of strange events which they claim took place after they encountered an odd patch of mist on the road not too far from here. They seem to be suffering from some form of psychological disturbance which resulted from this event. I am really at a loss as to what to do. Do you think you could help me?"

There was a short pause before Dr. Clarke answered.

"Have you thought of referring them to their GP?"

"Yes I have. They requested that I didn't speak to anyone else without their consent. To be honest, what they are reporting would leave their doctor flabbergasted. I suggested to them that you may be able to help outside of your official capacity."

Dr. Clarke spoke cautiously, though it was obvious that a degree of curiosity was arising within him.

"I may well be able to help if you give me a little more information, Mr. Bellamy."

"I can't really discuss this with you over the telephone. Could I come and see you as soon as possible, so I can then provide you with all the information I have. I have interviewed this couple on tape and I can make you a copy of this as well."

There was a sound of shuffling papers at the other end of the telephone.

"I don't have a great deal on today, Mr. Bellamy. I could come and visit you if you are not too far away."

Philip could hardly believe his luck. He gave details of his address to the psychologist, who seemed more than satisfied with the arrangements.

"Right, Mr. Bellamy. I should be over in about an hour or so, if that's okay with you."

"Okay, I'll see you then."

Philip replaced the receiver with hands that shook slightly. He was acutely aware of the reputation which his field of interest had with the scientific community. He knew that the psychologist had worked on cases before, but he had no guarantee that his views were the same now as they were two decades ago when he worked on the case which lay on the desk in front of him. Philip dismissed his thoughts as he began to rewind the tape that held the Morrison's interview. He would soon find out what Dr. Clarke's feelings for such things were.

Pamela and Alan worked their way through a simple meal without much enthusiasm. They felt oppressed by the familiar and hitherto welcome Sunday afternoon calm which had descended upon the little world of their cul-de-sac. This sense of detachment was heightened even further by the distant sounds of children playing in the fields behind them. Wendy was unusually silent and had to be told frequently to stop toying with her food during the meal. As they gratefully cleared up empty plates, Alan remembered the promise that he had made to Albert. He had usually managed to avoid visiting Pamela's parents in the past, but he now felt strangely in need of Albert's support and his wife's understanding. His suggestion of a visit caused Pamela to brighten considerably and they both found themselves hurrying to complete their lunch tasks. As Pamela busied herself with pots and pans, Alan approached Wendy, who was slumped in a chair facing the blank screen of the television.

"Anything wrong, love?"

She brushed a hair from her face and fixed her father with questioning eyes.

"There's something wrong with you and mum, isn't there?"

Alan feared that she would notice that something was wrong, but he secretly hoped that she would still be too young to read anything significant into her observations. He gazed down at his daughter for a second and realised that the girl who he had once known was fast becoming a beautiful young woman. In her he could see many of childhood's questions and insecurities melting away and being replaced slowly by an essence of something older and wiser. He realised that he could no longer depend upon her childish naiveté to shield her from the harsh realities which the future held for her. The knowledge that he could no longer protect her from an uncertain life as he had once done made him ache within, yet he still hoped that she could retain some of the energy and vitality which created a proud and strong child. He saw no sense in denying the fact, but decided against telling her the whole story.

"We've both been working very hard lately. You know that I've been doing the play and that mum has had various projects to deal with. That kind of thing can take its toll on anyone if it goes on for long enough and we've both had enough to be honest. Try not to worry about it; we'll both be okay in a while."

Wendy said nothing more, but it seemed to Alan that there were still questions which she didn't know how to ask. He tried to distract her from her train of thought.

"Me and your mum are going up to your grandma and granddad's for a bit now. Do you want to come with us?"

She shook her head apologetically.

"I feel really tired, dad. I don't fancy it at all."

He nodded as sympathetically with fatigue as anyone would be after the recent sleepless nights he had endured. He handed her the TV's remote control unit and paused to feel her brow, which was unusually warm. He allayed fears that she could be sickening for something as he studied her demeanour for a moment and saw that she looked perfectly well, if a little pale from her tiredness. He fought back the memories of his dreams, fearing the implications of what he would discover should he consider her part in the strange events of Friday night. He felt a new chill of fear when he considered for a moment his own sanity.

"Why not watch some TV for a while?"

"Maybe in a bit. I just want to be quiet for a moment."

He nodded understandingly

"Have you done all your homework?"

"I finished it on Friday."

He glanced at his watch.

"Look, it may be late before we get back so don't be frightened of making your own tea if you want some. There's plenty of stuff in the freezer if you don't want to cook anything special."

"Okay. I don't feel much like anything at the moment, but I'll get a bit of something later maybe."

Alan gave her one last concerned glance before he ruffled her hair and headed for the kitchen. His goodbye was acknowledged quietly as they both went through the door. Once they were in the car, Pamela turned to Alan with a concerned look on her face.

"Is Wendy alright? She seems a bit subdued today."

"She says she's a bit tired. It's not surprising when you consider what we've all been trough during the past few days. To be honest with you I'm very tired myself."

Pamela nodded her heartfelt agreement.

"You've looked better."

He looked her up and down.

"So have you."

"Yeah, I've also felt better."

He coaxed the car into life and reversed slowly down the drive. Pamela noticed the vehicle's sluggish nature immediately.

"When did this begin?"

"I first noticed it on Saturday morning, but it cut out just before we went into the mist, if you remember? Even though it seemed fine afterwards I wonder if this is the same fault. Perhaps it's something that took its time to have an effect on the car?"

Pamela's knowledge of cars was minimal, but even she realised that a major engine fault seemed to have affected the Passat. It seemed to her that the circumstances were slowly gathering and weaving an increasingly intricate maze of mystery around the events of Friday night. She felt an increasing sense of unease when she considered the events which had followed their encounter with the mist.

Alan paused at the junction with the main road for a moment before moving the car into the light traffic flow. He fought with the controls in his attempts to bring the vehicle up to cruising speed and eventually gave up in disgust. As a last resort, he angrily depressed the throttle to its stop and felt the engine falter into near silence. They were both unprepared for the shock of the sharp acceleration which immediately followed this and Alan backed off the power quickly. He depressed the pedal experimentally and felt the car surge again. He turned to Pamela in his amazement only to see her shrug her shoulders. He had to admit that he was now accepting things which would have seemed ludicrous to him just a few days ago. After their interview with Bellamy this morning, he didn't find it difficult to calmly accept the disappearance of what had appeared to be a major engine fault.

He followed the route to Albert and Margaret's house steadily, falling in with the sedate flow of light Sunday afternoon traffic which shared the road with him. They reached the small row of terraced cottages without incident and found Albert working his small patch of land which was bisected by the track that Alan was carefully negotiating. He waved at them as they approached and drew to a halt. Pamela hugged her father and then left him to join her mother, who was sitting in the front garden. Alan expected the crushing handshake and was surprised when Albert disregarded what time had turned into almost a ritual and instead offered him a can of beer from on icebox sited in the shade of the garden wall. He smiled as Alan took a deep swallow and wiped a hand across his mouth.

"You look like you needed that."

Alan nodded.

Albert allowed his daughter to wheel Margaret inside, pausing only to help her lift the chair over the step. Alan welcomed the quiet coolness of the cottage and followed Albert into the living room whilst Pamela worked with her mother in the kitchen. Albert gestured around himself at the room.

"Sorry about the mess. We weren't expecting visitors to be honest with you, but you're just as welcome as you ever were. What brings you into this neck of the woods anyway, Alan?"

Alan saw no point in evading the issue. He respected Albert too much to lie to him.

"We all had a bit of a weird experience on the way home on Friday night and it's shaken us up a bit to be honest. We hoped that you might be able to shed a little light on it."

Albert's expression changed as he slipped so easily back into habits acquired during a lifetime in the police force. He was immediately every inch the experienced police sergeant which he had been up until his retirement just a few years ago.

"What kind of experience?"

Alan felt uneasy under Albert's critical gaze and realised that what he was about to say might not be well received. His relief was obvious as he saw Pamela wheeling her mother back into the room. She positioned her near to the window and then began to pour tea from a large pot. Albert lifted his gaze to accommodate them all.

"What's this that Alan's been telling me about some trouble on the way home on Friday, Pamela? Are you all okay?"

Pamela shot a glance at Alan before turning to her father.

"We're fine. Just a little shaken up."

Alan paused to glance at the clock, but Albert understood his worry.

"Valerie won't be back to do the tea for another hour yet, so you're okay."

Alan began to speak, feeling as if the brief silence was his own.

"We left here at about half past nine on Friday night. Just outside the village on the road back to our house we came across a patch of green mist. The car began to play up a bit, but we passed through this and carried on home. We only realised that something had happened when we discovered what time it was when we got home. A journey which shouldn't have taken more than forty-five minutes took us almost three hours to complete."

Albert bridged his fingers and leant his chin on their peak, watching Alan attentively.

"Did you catch the time?"

"We rang the police station and the desk officer confirmed the time for us. We were tired, so we packed Wendy off to bed and followed her soon after. Neither of us got much sleep because we started to have these crazy dreams. This is when things started to get really odd. I think Pamela should carry on. To be honest, I don't think you'd believe me."

Albert turned to his daughter with questioning eyes and she hesitated before speaking.

"We... we both had this dream that we were in the mist and then the car was surrounded by strange figures. Wendy thought she saw a face at the window almost as soon as we entered the mist, but we both thought that it must have been a sheep which had got itself lost. The next thing we knew was that there was a massive thing hovering just above the road ahead of us with a ramp leading up into its interior. I think we must have blacked out at this point because the next thing I knew was that we were in this kind of room and standing by the car."

There was a short silence as she composed herself before continuing.

"The same figures that we had seen around the car were standing around us. They led us all away into different rooms and examined us before they allowed us to see each other again. I was so scared that I couldn't take much in, but I think they showed us a screen with some pictures on. The next thing I knew we were back in the car and driving back home."

She paused upon the completion of her story. When she spoke again, her voice held less of a nervous edge.

"I would have dismissed it as a nightmare, but Alan had a dream almost identical to mine. It felt so real. I've also got a mark where I dreamt the things touched me with things that looked like surgical instruments of some kind."

Neither of them realised it, but Albert's cool analytical expression had completely dissolved and been replaced by a look of sheer surprise, incredulity and disbelief. He spluttered in his amazement when he began to speak.

"That has got to be the stupidest thing I've ever heard. I don't know what was in that mist, but it sounds like it's turned your heads."

Anger filled Pamela's eyes and she protested despite herself.

"But we've been having these dreams for the last two nights, dad. You can't just say that we're imagining things. Something's wrong here. I know it."

Albert laughed.

"Calm down the both of you. I was only having a bit of a joke. Have you ever stopped to think about this? If everything went on whilst you were dreaming, then it stands to reason that that's all the whole thing is, a dream. I've heard of cases where whole communities can share the same dream, so I don't think it's unreasonable to say that you two may have been on the same wavelength for these past couple of days.

Alan leant nearer Albert and twisted his head to expose the small red mark behind his ear.

"I don't know how this got there, but it wasn't there on Friday morning. Pamela has a similar mark on her abdomen. We both dreamt that we were touched in these places."

Albert waved a dismissive hand at the mark.

"Haven't you heard of coincidence? Look, I'm not saying that you're lying, but don't you think you're both blowing this out of all proportion. Both of you should get a grip on yourselves."

Margaret reached out from her chair and rested a comforting hand on Pamela's arm.

"Look, love, I can remember when I've had dreams which made me afraid to walk in the dark for weeks after. I know that dreams can seem real, but try to calm

down a bit. This can't be real because things like this don't happen, except in those silly space wars film things."

Pamela snatched her hand away angrily and stood up.

"I was depending on you two for support. This thing is scaring the living daylights out of me."

She ran from the room and they all heard the outside door slam. Alan retrieved his coat from the arm of the sofa.

"I'm sorry about all of this, but she's not taking it very well. Neither of us has been sleeping at all since Friday."

Albert stood up to see him to the door and rested a comforting hand on his shoulder.

"It sounds like you've both been having a rough time. Try talking to her, she'll listen if you just give her time."

Alan saw no point in trying to reason with either of them. He suddenly discovered just how far he had pushed back the frontiers of his own acceptance. With this came the realisation that he was no longer the man he had been. This event had begun to change them both and his own sense of bewilderment was becoming more profound with each passing day. He said a half-hearted goodbye and left the house. Pamela was nowhere to be seen and Alan eventually picked her up half way down the narrow lane. She had been crying and her tears broke free again as she climbed into the car. She pushed away from Alan's comforting arms almost immediately and stared at him with wild, frightened eyes.

"What's happening to us, Alan?"

With his answer, he embodied the fear and bewilderment which they both shared.

"I don't know, love. I really don't know."

She fell into his arms again as the sobs began to wrack her body. As he held her, he thought about what Albert had said. It was the first time that he had considered events from that angle, but he had to admit that there was little solid, objective proof that the events which plagued them both now existed anywhere outside a strange, shared dream. He still favoured the explanation that they had become lost on the way home after they had been through the mist and had somehow become hypnotised by the highway whilst the hours rolled by. He knew a little about psychology and had heard of cases where people suffering from amnesia had created memories to fill the gaps in their conscious recollection of events. If this creation process had begun whilst they slept, then that would explain the dreams. He mentally retraced his steps and followed the line of reasoning again. He was surprised to find his explanation was actually convincing. He stemmed Pamela's sobs and captured her attention before explaining his thoughts to her. She shook her head slowly.

"That doesn't make any sense, Alan. There's no way that the mind would produce memories so dramatic that they would prevent a person from sleeping. We're going to have to face the facts sooner or later."

Alan averted his eyes from hers and allowed her to sit back in her seat.

"I'd rather it was later."

Pamela persevered.

"Something's happened and we don't know what. Whatever it is, it's something to do with that mist. We've spoken to Philip and he's working on it at the moment, so at least we're getting somewhere. This has happened to other people and as far as we know they've lived through it, so there's no reason to believe that we won't. Whatever the ultimate outcome of this, we're going to have to try to be strong, if not for us then for Wendy."

He started the engine and drove away without a word. His thoughtful silence persisted as they passed through the village and joined the main road. Pamela was momentarily surprised when they took an unexpected turning, but realisation dawned when she saw that Alan was following an arc of narrow country tracks, the final one of which rejoined the main road at a point just beyond the section where they had encountered the mist. She was secretly relieved at not having to pass through that area again. Alan finally spoke just before they entered their cul-de-sac.

"I don't think we should tell anybody else other than Philip about this. It's becoming easier for us to accept because we have to live with it, but I've realised now that this will always seem strange to other people. We can't afford to let this get out because we've both got jobs to keep."

Pamela nodded in agreement.

"I think we can trust Philip not to say anything."

"We have his word. If his colleagues are as professional as he is, then we don't have to worry."

******

PART THREE

INVESTIGATION AND REGRESSION

CHAPTER SEVEN

IN CONVERSATION WITH DOCTOR CLARKE

Philip Bellamy fed another sheet of paper into his printer and watched it begin to mindlessly spew out line after line of characters. He had decided to print three copies of the now complete transcript in order that they could all follow the recorded interview. Just as he stole a quick glance at his watch, he heard the bell which was connected to the garage's back door sound. He descended the stairs and was not fully prepared for the person that greeted him as he opened the door.

Dr. Henry Clarke did not possess the diminutive size which characterised many of his fellow scientists and his height was accompanied by a solid bodily build which the passing years had not managed to bend. Philip was aware of his age, but could see that he had the appearance of someone considerably younger, possessing a healthy complexion and full head of light brown hair. His features were as sharp as any he had seen, honed almost to perfection as if by the power of the mind which sat behind bright and articulate steely grey eyes.

Philip was also surprised when he saw that the doctor was dressed casually and fashionably with not a trace of tweed waistcoat or small glasses with circular frames. He instead appeared to favour a modern pair of bifocals which sat easily on the bridge of his nose. He stood on the doorstep and made no move to enter the building until Philip invited him in. Dr. Clarke shook the proffered hand then followed Philip as he led the way up to the flat. He settled himself into an armchair and gratefully accepted a cup of tea. When Philip had seated himself, he began to speak.

"I have been doing a little of my own checking, Philip, and I must say that your credentials as a UFO researcher are impeccable."

Philip could have groaned. He had deliberately avoided any reference to UFOs during his conversation with Dr. Clarke and had not imagined that he would have any interest in the field at all. The psychologist read his barely noticeable change in expression and he allowed himself a genuine, benevolent smile.

"Don't worry, I knew that you were speaking about a UFO-related event almost as soon as you began to tell the story of your two witnesses."

"Then what has made you get involved? I understood that you had been involved in other cases as a consultant only?"

He nodded.

"That's true, but a great deal has gone on since then and now. I recently met one of the people involved in a case which I had worked on some years ago. She reported an experience very similar to the one you are dealing with now. I must confess that the case was investigated poorly by all, including myself. As a result, I think that this person is experiencing a psychological disturbance which could well have been avoided if I had taken a little more time to research the subject. You could say that I am becoming involved this time in order that the past is not repeated again. As to the subject of UFOs, you know that I care little about that subject and know even less. I believe that you are a graduate of the later schools of thought which tends to see these experiences as being completely separate from the UFO phenomenon. This is what I favour, as I believe that we are dealing with is a predominantly psychological problem."

He paused for a moment and drank some of his tea. He looked at Philip and the investigator was intrigued to see that his eyes twinkled with a powerful and recently awakened interest. He smiled ruefully.

"Cutting through all of that lot, you would also be correct in drawing the conclusion that I am also absolutely fascinated."

Philip also grinned and began to relax in the doctor's presence. He had not been looking forward to continuing his little deception right up until he played the interview and all was revealed. As he calmed himself, his mind cleared and he turned to the task in hand. He handed a copy of the transcript to Dr. Clarke.

"That's the interview with the two witnesses. It was conducted in their home, as you will see, and there was virtually no time for preparation in either case. I don't know whether it will be of any use to you, considering your field of interest, but what I planned to do was play the interview when Andrew Howarth arrives and then discuss the events later?"

Dr. Clarke looked at him questioningly.

"Andrew Howarth? Isn't that the editor of the local newspaper?"

Philip looked a little uncomfortable.

"Well... yes. He's also a member of the same group which I am involved with and I couldn't really exclude him from the investigation. I also thought that we could keep the story down more effectively if we involved him and impressed upon him the importance of silence for the moment."

"All the same, I think it would have been better if he had not been involved. If there is one group of people who display a remarkable lack of understanding, then it must be the press."

"I agree. Try not to worry, Dr. Clarke. I'm sure that we can trust him."

The psychologist nodded as if satisfied.

"Okay, and call me Henry, for heaven's sake. I thought that I would only be tagged 'doctor' during working hours. I can assure you that there is nothing illustrious about the title after thirty-five years."

Before Philip could respond to this, the door bell rang again. He left the room and returned a few moments later, accompanied by Andrew Howarth. The reporter was a small man, overweight and gasping from the climb up the short flight of stairs from the workshop. He cast narrow eyes about himself and allowed his gaze to settle on Dr. Clarke. His eyes widened and Dr. Clarke stood up and extended a hand.

"I'm Dr. Henry Clarke. I understand that you are Mr. Howarth."

Howarth's handshake was weak and it seemed that the social pleasantries were already boring him. He sat down without invitation and flicked his briefcase open. Despite the heat, he wore a heavy sweater and would not allow Philip to take his coat from him. The psychologist studied Howarth as he began to sort through his papers. The precise and rapid manner in which he assembled his micro dictation machine and loaded it with tape dispelled any initial impressions of the foolishness which his appearance suggested. He finally spoke.

"I didn't know that Philip was involving a psychologist on this case. This isn't standard practice within the group."

Dr. Clarke recognised the challenge and deflected it with ease.

"From what Mr. Bellamy has told me, this does not appear to be a normal case."

Howarth returned to his preparations and spoke as he shuffled a pile of papers.

"It looks like there may well be something newsworthy here, then. It's about time we had a bit of excitement around here. The last interesting thing in this paper was World War Two."

Dr. Clarke's dislike of the man intensified. Philip rejoined them after preparing the interview tape for playback. He pushed a copy of the interview transcript over the table towards Howarth.

"I'll play back the audio of the interview to supplement these. I think it will add more depth and will give both of you the opportunity to begin to build up a coherent picture of events leading up to this incident."

He flicked a control on the tape deck and settled down as the interview began. During the course of the playback, he glanced up at Howarth and Dr. Clarke. The latter appeared deep in concentration, studying his transcript and quite obviously keeping pace with the tape, pausing only to make notes. The reporter was recording the proceedings and scribbling furtively, his sweeping pencil strokes suggesting that he was occasionally moving to a picture which was sharing the page with his notes. He allowed a short silence after the tape had finished before speaking.

"I have to admit that I'm baffled by this, which is primarily why I have called upon you as you both possess the expertise which will allow us to look into this further. Do you have any opinions?"

Howarth grinned and held up his paper, the drawing which he had been working on was a poor interpretation of one of the beings which both Alan and Pamela had described during the interview. Philip picked up other references to 'spaceships' and 'flying saucers' as he glanced at the notes above the drawing. He looked to Dr. Clarke who laid down his pen calmly and paused to study his last short note before looking up and addressing both of them.

"I haven't formed any opinions as yet, but I do think it would be a good idea if this was kept quiet until we have looked into it further. The obvious traumas which are present in both witnesses could be deepened still further if they are subject to ridicule or if they encounter disbelief in any form."

Philip nodded.

"Yeah. I agree with you there. I've already asked them not to speak about their experience. I was aware that problems may be generated if they are subject to a great deal of attention, but I also thought that the memory of the event may remain more lucid within their minds if they didn't tell their story too often."

Howarth clicked his tape recorder to a halt and laughed with incredulity.

"I can't believe you two. We've got stories of alien kidnappings right on our doorstep and you want to keep it quiet! This is the biggest thing since sliced bread round here and it would make one hell of an article."

Philip's face darkened and his voice became stern.

"I've already asked you to keep this quiet, Andrew. You above anyone else should know just how damaging publicity can be at times like this."

The reporter continued undaunted, eyes shining as the article unfolded in his mind.

"But we could ask other people who have been kidnapped to come forward. Surely it would be better if we had a few cases to look at?"

Philip moved to reply but Dr. Clarke spoke first.

"Publicising one case would be bad enough, but subjecting a whole batch of them to journalistic license would be unforgivable. You don't appear to be able to grasp the fact that we are dealing with people who have had a deeply disturbing

experience. The last thing they need right now is a bunch of you people descending on their doorstep and asking all sorts of questions about aliens and spaceships. If you publish details of this case before the investigation is complete, you could do untold damage."

Howarth sat back in his chair and waved his hands in front of him as if he was attempting to block the onslaught of Dr. Clarke's verbal barrage.

"Okay, okay, keep your hair on. I just thought there may be an article here, that's all."

Philip slammed his pencil down on the table.

"No article, Andrew, and that's final. I've allowed you to record the interview in full because you are a member, but that has to be where your interest remains for the moment."

Dr. Clarke consulted his watch.

"I'm afraid that you two will have to excuse me. My wife will be most upset if I miss dinner again and I have also got a great deal of work to do. I should be most grateful if you could allow me to speak with the witnesses as soon as possible, Philip."

The investigator stood to see him to the door.

"I was thinking of tomorrow night, if that fitted in with you."

He nodded immediately.

"Yes, that would be wonderful. I'll call here at around five tomorrow, if that's okay with you."

Philip shook the doctor's hand and smiled.

"That would be great. I'll look forward to seeing you."

Dr. Clarke took hold of his briefcase and left with a curt nod in Howarth's direction. As soon as he left, the reporter stood up.

"I've got to be going as well."

Philip caught his eye as he headed for the door.

"You've got that, haven't you?"

"What?"

"You know what! Nothing has to go in the paper about this until the witnesses give it their okay."

Howarth averted his eyes.

"Okay, okay. Don't get so uptight. You know you can trust me."

He left without another word. Philip moved to his packed bookcase and removed a book entitled *Elementary Psychology*. He leafed through it thoughtfully.

******

CHAPTER EIGHT

HOW TO COPE?

A telephone sounded shrilly in the darkened kitchen. Alan left his chair almost impulsively and reached through the door to snatch the receiver from its cradle. There was a short pause after he announced the number before a familiar voice began to speak.

"Alan? It's Philip here. I'm just ringing to thank you for your hospitality this morning and also tell you that I have spoken with my colleagues and we'd like to interview you both again at some time in the near future."

Alan paused for a moment.

"Just who are these people, Philip?"

"One of them is called Henry Clarke. He's a psychologist and he's had experience of dealing with this kind of thing. The other one is Andrew Howarth, the editor of the local paper."

Pamela looked up in surprise as Alan's raised voice broke through the silence of the living room. She stood and hurried to the phone, grasping his shoulders with concern. He repeated his last sentence when Philip did not speak.

"I thought you told us to keep this quiet. Nobody gave you permission to give this to the papers."

He listened carefully and heard the telltale hiss of the phone connection. Philip had not cut him off. The investigator finally spoke.

"I was worried that you might say that. I don't want any publicity either, but I had to involve him. The problem is that he's been a member of the local group which I am involved with for some time. If he found out about this from some other source, he would waste no time in going to press and you'd have no say in the matter. At least by involving him, we can manage to keep him and this story under control."

Alan's anger abated somewhat. He began to feel guilty about unloading his insecurities onto Philip.

"I can see the problem that you have, but I'm still not happy. As far as another interview goes, I don't think we'll have any objections at all. I'd like to make it as soon as possible, if you can manage that. We're both ready to get this thing sorted out now."

Philip sounded optimistic.

"How about tomorrow night then?"

"That would be fine. Say around 7pm."

He mouthed 'seven' at Pamela who nodded. He brought the receiver back to his mouth again.

"Seven will be fine with us. Do you want us to make any preparations?"

"No. It will just be an interview like I did with you both this morning."

"Okay, see you then."

Alan replaced the receiver and turned back to Pamela who had a questioning look on her face.

"Just Philip. He's spoken with two guys. One's a psychologist who knows a bit about this and the other one's Andrew Howarth. Apparently, he's a member of a local UFO group and Philip was worried that he might find out about this and splash it all over the papers. He thinks that getting him involved might help to keep things quiet."

Pamela simply nodded in agreement.

"That's just what we don't want. It could make us a laughing stock if this gets out. Just look at what went on at mum and dads today. That looks like the average kind of reaction we can expect to encounter."

She paused for a moment and Alan saw that her bottom lip was beginning to tremble. She pulled him to her as sobs burst forth.

"Christ, Alan! What the hell's going on? What's happening to us? "

He comforted her as best he could as she cried, but the knowledge that he couldn't answer her questions brought with it a cold fear of the unknown such as he had not felt since the days when his childhood terrors made him fight to stay awake in his darkened room. He could once again feel the shadows begin to stretch from the darkest corner and take on a substance of evil that he once thought could not exist outside of the horror novels which he had read as a boy.

At that moment he felt as uncertain and lonely as he had ever done. It seemed to him that the tidy little world of calm and steady normality that he had once inhabited was now breaking up in the face of this incomprehensible and devastating assault. He was so uncomfortable with the knowledge that he would have cried if there had been someone for him to lean on. Pamela moved away from his encircling arms and sat down wearily.

"I'm tired, I'm going to bed."

They caught each other's eyes and fear passed between them. Neither knew what another night held for them. Each was on the point of praying for peace and calm through the night, but both feared a return of the nightmares. The wave of tiredness which washed over Alan at that moment helped him make up his mind. He was going to take a chance despite what might happen. He helped Pamela from the stool and switched off the lights before half carrying her up the stairs. Wendy had already gone to bed and no light shone beneath her door. Alan opened it quietly and heard her steady breathing. He was once again thankful that she was not affected. They both undressed and collapsed into bed, falling asleep almost instantly.

The mist closed around them and faces began to peer through the window. One of them held a giant needle and inserted it right through the window into Alan's head. It seemed to him that it raked his very nerve endings, causing pain which he had not imagined he could feel. Images became confused and rolled over each other at an increasing rate until it seemed that he moved through a ghastly psychedelic confusion. He could feel the desperation in a billion unrealised dreams and the hopelessness of countless wasted lives. The feelings began to bombard him, taking on their own peculiar form of incomprehensible procession through his tortured mind until finally reaching a crescendo such that he had thought he could never have experienced. The energy threatened to tear his very being apart fibre by fibre and consume every one in a white-hot furnace of tortured souls. In his agony, he gave each one a voice and cried for them all.

Wild eyes snapped open and stared at the darkened ceiling. Pamela flicked on a light and Alan turned to stare at her for a moment before his mind became fully conscious and he sank back against the pillows, his eyes clouding once more. They held each other for what seemed an age before moving apart. Pamela looked at him worriedly.

"You nearly woke the entire street with that. What on earth is happening, Alan? You look scared out of your mind."

Alan stared in silence at the soft glow cast by the light bulb for a moment.

"Don't ever ask me to go to sleep again. I'm going to make some coffee and wait for the sun to rise."

He pushed the covers back, but allowed himself to be restrained from moving further by Pamela's hand on his shoulder. Her voice was gentle but concerned.

"What did you dream about? Was it about Friday night again?"

He turned to her and she saw the answer in his eyes.

"That dream was the most frightening experience I have ever had, Pamela. To be honest I'm scared out of my wits. Any more of that and I'd have been heading for a strait-jacket."

He left the bed and grabbed his dressing gown before leaving the room. Pamela heard him descending the stairs softly. Though it seemed to her that she had no more tears, she began to cry once more in her own misery and wretched fear.

******

CHAPTER NINE

MOUNTING PRESSURE

Wendy was not surprised to find both her parents already up when she rose at 7am. Alan and Pamela did their best to hide their worry and tiredness from their daughter, but they could not even begin to disguise their haggard looks and drooping shoulders. Both noticed Wendy shooting furtive glances at them from time to time as she poured milk onto her breakfast cereal. She brought the bowl over to the table where they sat and fixed concerned eyes on her father.

"Are you going to school today, dad, or do you want me to catch the bus?"

Alan seemed surprised by the question; his mind too deadened by tiredness to notice even Wendy's thinly-veiled reference to his apparent poor health.

"Of course I'm going to school, love. Do you want to catch the bus anyway? I'll give you the fare if you want."

Wendy shook her head as she munched away at her tasty breakfast cereal.

"No, I'll come with you, if that's okay."

He nodded.

"No problem."

Alan and Pamela dressed together and shared their uncertainties about the coming day. The realisation that they would have to once again face familiar people dawned simultaneously and they worried at their parting and at the events which might follow. Monday mornings had formally heralded an air of optimism and enthusiasm for them both, but they now found themselves fearing the onslaught of the outside world which they felt had altered forever.

Ignoring breakfast, they both left the house quietly, taking a long private moment for their ritual leaving kiss, which, this morning, became a passionate embrace they hoped would not end. Alan drove slowly down the cul-de-sac at Pamela's walking pace and they stared at each other for long minutes until Pamela took the path across the fields and became lost behind the wall.

Alan joined the familiar main road and fell in with the light commuter traffic, responding again to an almost subconscious urge to avoid the area where they had encountered the fog. His detour added to the duration of his journey and he discovered, to his consternation, that they were fifteen minutes late when he finally reached the gates of the school. He said a quick goodbye to Wendy as they parted in the yard before hurrying into the building.

He paused once he was through the doors, fighting to remember where his first class of the morning was to be held. The sounds of laughter and loud chatter filtering down the stairway towards him served as a rude reminder that he had not even taken his registration class yet. He wearily threw himself up the stairs and followed the long corridor to his classroom at its far end. He paused once more as he reached the door, surprised and disturbed by the silence which he realised had fallen. He slowly entered the room and was shocked to see the figure of Sidney Potter, the school's headmaster, surveying the now silent and terrified class with dark eyes. He spoke in precisely clipped tones which held within them contempt for the children which he now faced.

"I am disgusted at the noise which I heard when I entered this room! Absence of your form teacher is no excuse for such behaviour! If there is a repeat of this under any circumstances then I shall ensure that you are all detained after school for the rest of the week!"

He turned and saw Alan standing at the door. He left his position at the head of the desk and walked over to him.

"I trust you will deal with this, Mr. Morrison?"

The challenge made Alan uneasy.

"Yes I will, Mr. Potter."

The headmaster nodded curtly and left the room. Alan clearly heard his whispered words as he brushed past him.

"I'll see you in my office at morning break, Mr. Morrison."

He took Alan's agreement for granted and knew that he dared not protest in front of his class. He shot one more dark look at the terrified children before he turned on his heel and left the room. Alan kicked the door shut and sat down at the desk. He surveyed the class wearily for a moment and saw a few puzzled looks on their faces. He smiled reassuringly and looked towards Julie.

"Well, what was all that about?"

Julie reddened as she realised she had been singled out, but spoke with the self-assurance of a wronged person despite this.

“Sir, we were just chatting and Mr. Potter walked in. He went mad at all of us for nothing, sir.”

He nodded understandingly and turned to address the whole class.

“Okay. Despite that, what Mr. Potter says still stands. If there is a repeat of this morning’s performance, then detentions all round will be the only answer. Just because I’m a bit late that doesn’t mean that you lot can start swinging from the light fittings. You’ll get me into trouble as well as yourselves. Have you all got that?”

Some nodded; others merely looked at their shoes or fiddled with pens. Despite this, he was satisfied that he had dispelled the uneasiness which the headmaster’s entrance had brought about. He glanced at his watch.

“Okay, you’re all going to be late if you don’t get a move on. I’ll take both registers this afternoon, so don’t any of you think you can go nicking off this lunchtime because you’ll get caught.”

The momentarily subdued noise began again as the children started gathering their bags together and chatted again. The noise grated on Alan’s frayed nerves and he gritted his teeth as the pain in his head worsened. As the torture continued, he clenched his fists and finally brought both of them down on the desk.

"QUIET!!”

Thirty-two heads snapped round in surprise and stared at their red-faced and unshaven teacher. Their conversation began again a moment later, but barely rose above a nervous whisper as they continued to file out. Alan consulted his timetable and was relieved when he realised that he wasn’t teaching during the two periods between registration and morning break. He surveyed the piles of unmarked books surrounded by the general disarray of the classroom. The volume of work wearied him further and he chose instead to pull a paperback novel from his open briefcase. He was trying to make some sense of the words when a soft knock came at the door. He turned as it was opened softly and Brian Wilcox walked in. As soon as he was through the door, he seemed instantly surprised at Alan’s appearance.

“You look disgusting. What the hell have you been drinking?”

Alan let his head fall into his hands.

“I wish I had been drinking.”

Brian’s eyes narrowed with concern and his shaggy eyebrows seemed to bridge the gap above his nose.

"What's up, Alan? You're not yourself at all."

"You wouldn't even be able to begin believing me, Brian. I can assure you of that."

"Well, whatever, I've just come to plug you into the grapevine. I don't know what's gone on with you and Pamela this weekend, but it was noticed that you were very late and very grumpy this morning. I've also heard that you've had the summons from Adolf himself so you'd better buck your ideas up pretty soon because he's not impressed by normal human depression at all."

Alan looked up at him again with clouded eyes.

"Adolf can go and take a bloody running jump for all I care. If he gives me any hassle, then I'll tell him that. This is the first time I've been late for seven years and I can't see how he can come down on me for that."

Brian's look of concern deepened.

"If you go in there with both guns blazing, you'll find yourself out on your ear in no time at all. Haven't you worked out by now that Potter doesn't like you?"

Alan had noticed that Potter's attitude towards him had been disapproving for some time, but his love of teaching and his natural optimism had allowed him to disregard the implications of this. Now that both enjoyment and optimism had left him, the realisation that his relationship with the headmaster was strained to a degree dawned and his misery encroached still further. He nodded weakly.

"It doesn't look too good."

Brian shrugged and opened the door again.

"Perhaps not. All you can do is go in there with plenty of 'yes sirs' and 'no sirs' and hope that he feels good enough from you're crawling to want to keep you on. I credited you with more intelligence than this, Alan. Don't go and blow it all now."

The door closed with a slam. Alan lapsed into melancholy thought and stared out of the window for what seemed like an age. He gradually became aware of his surroundings once more as noise from the corridor beyond filtered through into the silent classroom. He glanced at his watch and was surprised to discover that an hour had passed since Brian's departure. He stood wearily and composed himself as best he could before leaving the room and heading for the headmaster's office.

His knocks upon the large door went ignored for some time before Potter's clipped voice broke through the noise from the playground.

“Enter.”

Alan took a deep breath and thrust the door open. Sydney Potter was seated at an immense desk which was crudely constructed along the same lines as its smaller counterparts which lined the classrooms of the school he ruled. He was a man who seemed to be inexplicably linked with his surroundings, even if only in the sense that his complexion matched the pale grey shades of the school’s walls and his features and figure matched the building’s sparse and angular appearance.

“I originally asked you to see me in order to explain your lateness, Mr. Morrison. I now find that I have to bring another, possibly more serious, matter to your attention. It would appear that your behaviour has already been noted as being out of character with only just over an hour of the day gone. I should like an explanation for this.”

Alan allowed the silence to settle for a moment as he collected his thoughts. As he began to speak, Potter made an exaggerated series of gestures which resulted in a precise bridge of long fingers upon which he rested his angular chin in a parody of interest.

“To be honest with you, sir, I’ve had quite a rough weekend. I don’t know whether this has filtered back to you as well, but Pamela and I are going through quite a rough patch at the moment and we’ve not had much sleep this weekend. I expected a decent night’s sleep last night, but didn’t get one, so I was late this morning as a result.”

The headmaster angled his head in question.

“And do you consider this to be an adequate excuse for your behaviour this morning?”

“I don’t have an excuse, sir, but I would say that the events of the last few days should be taken into consideration.”

It seemed to Alan that the man’s hard and cold eyes softened as the next question formed in his mind.

“How long have these problems been going on for, Alan?”

“We’ve always been committed to our jobs and this has caused problems since day one, but we’ve always managed to overcome them before. To be honest, it feels as if things have been building for a long time.”

The hardness returned to Potter's eyes.

"I've no interest in your problems, Mr. Morrison. If you are having problems with your wife, then go and see a marriage guidance counsellor. I feel it only fair to tell you that the governors will be meeting shortly and staffing levels will be discussed. I will be forced to put forward names for possible transfer. I have not made my list yet, but I am currently compiling a directory of possibilities. Your name was not destined to be one of them, but I am afraid your behaviour this morning and your lax attitudes which have persisted over the past few months have helped me change my mind."

Alan stared at him with surprise.

"What do you mean by 'lax attitudes'? My grades have been the best in the school for some time and you know that I can get results from the kids."

The headmaster picked up a pencil and rolled it thoughtfully between his thumbs and index fingers.

"Getting results is not all that is required of a teacher within my school, Mr. Morrison, and I am sure that you realise this. There also has to be respect for the establishment which was been built up before you over decades. You appear to hold such things as tradition in contempt and your attitude quite clearly demonstrates this. As such, I believe that you would serve a more progressive establishment better than you serve this one."

Alan became angry, despite the imposing presence of his superior.

"So you're kicking me out because I don't wear a pinstriped suit, eh? Look, I know there's a great deal more to this than just respect for tradition. The whole top and bottom of it is that you just don't like me and you never have done. You think you've got this situation wrapped up now, don't you? Well you're very wrong, because the first place that I am going when I leave here is the union representative. It's their tradition to take a very dim view of victimisation, as I'm sure you know."

He immediately regretted his outburst as Potter leaned across his desk and reduced his voice to a threatening whisper.

"You will go straight to the class which you should be teaching when you leave this room, Mr. Morrison. If I have one more report of lateness, then I will have you disciplined by the same union that you are now contemplating involving and I can assure you that you will not want that. You also don't appear to realise that transferring you is not the only option before me. I can put before the board with the recommendation that you are not offered another post as you are quite clearly unsuited to the teaching profession. Something of that magnitude will spread down the grapevine very rapidly, Mr. Morrison, I can assure you of that. Finding another post will then be made very difficult."

His eyes darkened still further.

"Do I make myself clear, Mr. Morrison?"

Alan nodded.

"You do."

"Then get out of here and fulfil your responsibilities to your pupils." Alan left without a word.

******

CHAPTER TEN

THE NEXT APPOINTMENT

Pamela threw her pen aside and looked in disgust at yet another mistake. The atmosphere within the small office oppressed her and it seemed to her that the walls were visibly closing in as immense black clouds rolled down from the hills to the north and obscured the sun. She watched as light drizzle quickly became heavy rain which blew against the window in noisy sheets. In the same instant that she became aware of a presence behind her, she was jabbed in the shoulder with the butt of a pen. She turned angrily and was met by the grinning, bearded face of Andrew Gibson.

"I think I'm working on much the same project as you are at the moment. How about extending some of your co-operation in this direction then maybe we can be finished in time to take a long lunch. What do you think?"

Pamela looked back to her papers in disgust.

"Why don't you just forget the long lunch?"

The rebuff served only to broaden Gibson's smile.

"Come on. I know its Monday morning, but there's no need to be like that with me of all people."

Pamela stared at her papers for a moment longer before turning to Gibson with eyes that blazed with anger.

"Why don't you just get lost, you little creep! You really disgust me with talk like that! Are you so stupid that you haven't got the message or would you like me to have my husband spell it out for you? Just go and finish your work and forget about lunch because I'd rather eat in an abattoir!"

The force of her words appeared to physically propel Gibson towards the door. Before he left the room he screwed up a page from his notepad and threw it at her.

"What the hell's up with you anyway? Is it your time of the month of something, you miserable sod?"

"GET OUT!"

As her scream reverberated down the corridor, she became aware of another presence behind her. She turned and saw Janice Burrows looking at her quizzically.

Janice conformed more to the classic image of the social worker than Pamela could ever hope to. She was broader and less shapely and her light brown hair refused to hold onto the perm which had been forced upon it some time ago. Her natural attractiveness was less sophisticated than Pamela's, stemming more from her kindly nature and constant smile which seemed firmly embedded into a face which held bright eyes and round, rosy cheeks. She favoured loose, practical clothes which tended to disguise her figure rather than attempt to flatter it. Despite obvious outward differences, however, Pamela and Janice shared many common beliefs and traits of character and they had been friends since their first meeting many years ago.

Janice dragged a chair away from the table and sat down next to Pamela.

"What was that all about, Pam?"

Pamela massaged her temples with forefinger and thumb as she continued to stare non-comprehendingly at the books in front of her.

"I'm just sick of that little creep making passes at me."

Janice leant her chin on the table and looked at Pamela.

"You don't usually act like that. Is there anything wrong?"

Pamela shielded her eyes and looked away.

"I'm just going through a bit of a bad patch with Alan. I don't really want to talk about it."

Janice's voice held an understanding which only true friends can enjoy.

"Okay. Don't hesitate to give me a shout if you want to get it off your chest, though. I'll have a word with Gibson as well; get him to lay off you a bit."

Pamela ran a hand through her hair and nodded weakly as she did so.

"Okay, thanks, Janice."

Janice left the room and quietly closed the door. Pamela was thankful for her departure as the first tear dropped from her cheek and fell onto the book's open page.

The rugged landscape seemed to brace itself in the face of the advancing rain which soaked its barren moor lands and swept down its rugged valleys in damp sheets. Animals in the fields clustered around any available shelter and made their own where there was none. The windswept day pitted itself against Alan and Pamela and progressed agonisingly slowly, yet it seemed to be in a strange, grudging sympathy with their moods. Pamela sat and stared at the clock as its hands slowly ground round its sparse face. She felt within those interminable workings there lay the answer to her questions. Her conscious mind could not place the events of Friday into any chronological order and yet she felt that this was not due solely to her disorientation. A sneaking suspicion that they had been confronted by something completely alien in shape, form and action also lay at the back of her mind and subtly coloured her perceptions and thoughts. She reached the end of an unrewarding day with relief and left the office on the dot of 5pm, despite the wind and rain which would have normally had her ringing Alan asking him to pick her up. She recognised the figure of Janice at the bus stop and joined her beneath a huge umbrella. Pamela placed a steadying hand on its wooden handle and turned to her with a smile.

"I'm sorry about this morning, Janice. Things just got on top of me a bit."

Janice squinted to look at her as she turned her face into the wind.

"Its okay, Pam. I know what you're going through at the moment. Don't forget that I've been there myself a couple of time and I know that it's not fun."

A gust of wind turned the umbrella inside out and the rain began to wet them immediately. Pamela gasped at its onslaught and saw the welcoming light of the Rope and Anchor out of the corner of her eye. She pointed to the inn's closed door.

"Why don't we get out of this and have a drink?"

Janice's grin broadened.

"Are you buying?"

"Whatever you want."

"That's what I like to hear!"

Both women dashed across the road and relinquished the umbrella's decreased protection at the last possible moment before pulling the door open and entering the pub. The warmth of the open fire dispelled their cold the instant the door was closed and the air of calmness was a welcome respite to them after the storm's ferocity.

Janice wrestled her umbrella closed as she took her seat in a corner booth and made space for Pamela as she arrived with the drinks. Janice noted with surprise that one of the glasses held a generous double measure of whiskey, which Pamela downed in one mouthful, grimacing at the taste as the liquid burned her throat.

"What the hell is up with you, Pam? I haven't seen you drink like that since last Christmas."

She noticed that Pamela's empty glass was shaking despite the fact she held it tightly with both of her cold-reddened hands. Janice laid one of her hands on Pamela's to steady them.

"Go on, Pam. Don't upset yourself for the sake of bottling it all up."

Pamela's shaking lessened as she began to speak. She related Friday night's event, pausing occasionally to steady herself before continuing from the point she had reached. Her voice was soft and lacking in the emotion which a degree of acceptance had now negated to some extent. Janice was shocked by Pamela's weary appearance when she finally completed her story. She found the events which had been related impossible to comprehend, yet alone to believe. Her training refused to allow her to draw any immediate conclusions, however, compelling her instead to address Pamela on her own level of belief. Her colleague had quite clearly not been lying and it was enough for Janice. She took a sip from her glass of lager.

"I won't pretend to understand any of what you have just said, but I think you should find someone who knows something about this kind of thing and tell them what you have told me. You know that I can't do anything in this case beyond listen to you, but I'll do what I can to find someone who can."

Pamela slowly turned the empty glass on its base with her index fingers.

"We've already spoken to Philip Bellamy, the guy who owns the garage here. He deals with this kind of thing and he's set up a meeting with a psychologist for us tonight. Apparently this Dr. Clarke has looked into cases like this before and has had a vast amount of experience in the field in general."

Janice nodded.

"I've heard of him. I think I read one of his books years ago, if I remember, all about altered states of consciousness and things like that. It was a bit deep for me, but he seemed to make sense."

Pamela pushed her glass away and prepared to rise. Their eyes met for a moment and Janice realised with surprise that Pamela's were filled with fear and uncertainty.

"Well, I hope he knows what he's doing. I've got to give Alan a ring to get him to pick me up. It looks like the bus has been and gone."

Janice looked at her watch in surprise.

"I've got to get a shift on myself. Now, Pamela, before I go, I want you to listen to me. If there's anything I can do for you then don't hesitate to call me, day or night."

The two women embraced for a moment.

"Thanks, Janice. Thanks for understanding and thanks for not trying to explain it all away."

Janice shook her head.

"No way would I even begin to attempt to explain that lot, Pamela. I just hope that this Dr. Clarke can."

Pamela was heartfelt in her agreement.

"So do I, Janice. So do I."

Pamela watched her leave as she called Alan on the pub's payphone. As the ponderous local exchange made the noisy connection, a profound feeling of relief descended upon her. Janice had been the only person other than Philip who had listened to her story and had not attempted to draw conclusions. Her calm acceptance of the events impressed Pamela and she felt that she could now approach the evening's meeting with renewed confidence. A distant phone began to ring and its receiver was lifted almost immediately by Alan.

"Hi. It's Pamela. Do you think you could come and pick me up? I'm at the Rope and Anchor in the village."

"No problem. Look, Wendy's been invited over to Julie's for tea and I think it might be a good idea if we let her go. What do you think?"

The weariness in Alan's voice alarmed her. It sounded as if he had aged considerably since they had parted that morning. She brought her mouth closer to the receiver and created added privacy by cupping her remaining hand over it.

"I was hoping we would be able to get her out of the way before they arrive, that looks like the ideal opportunity."

"Okay, I'll take her over there first and then come and pick you up. I should be with you in about a quarter of an hour."

Pamela shoved another coin into the telephone's moneybox.

"Okay. I'll throw a quick tea together when I get home."

Alan replaced the receiver without any acknowledgement.

CHAPTER ELEVEN

REGRESSIVE HYPNOSIS

Philip Bellamy extracted himself from the engine compartment of the Triumph as an unexpected knock on the garage's back door reverberated round the near-silent building. He opened it curiously and glanced at his watch as Dr. Clarke's apologetic face appeared.

"I'm sorry, Philip. I know I am early, but I was hoping we may be able to have a short discussion before we go onto the home of the witnesses."

Philip hurriedly wiped his fingers clean on his overalls and shook Dr. Clarke's proffered hand.

"No problem. I was wondering whether I was running late, to be honest with you. If you'd like to come in, I'll get out of this lot."

He led Dr. Clarke up to the flat and changed hurriedly into a casual outfit of jeans, loose shirt and sweater. As he entered the room, he noticed that the psychologist had an earnest look on his face. He began to speak almost immediately as Philip sat down.

"I think I've already told you that I have dealt with cases like this before?"

Philip nodded and motioned for the doctor to continue. He took the cue and spoke again.

"I was reviewing one such case last night in order to refresh my memory and quite a few interesting facts which I had failed to recall came to light."

Dr. Clarke pulled a sheaf of papers from his briefcase and quickly sorted through them before extracting the one which he required. It was a photocopy of an aged newspaper clipping which bore the headline 'LOCAL MAN MEETS ALIENS'. He began to speak again.

"I won't waste time with the details here, but I think you can see that this case attracted adverse media publicity, which eventually resulted in the alienation of the witness. In this case, the reporter in question was not actually involved in the investigation, but he did have a passing interest in UFOs and considered the case to be newsworthy. The case still remains partially un-investigated as a result of this."

As Philip scanned the body of the article, realization dawned. He looked up at Dr. Clarke as he returned the paper to him.

"And you're worried about Andrew Howarth's involvement with the case? I understand your fears, but I can assure you that he's as good as his word and he's given me his word that none of this will be released until we all okay it. I know the press can be unpredictable at the best of times, but I've worked with Andrew before and I know that he will look before leaping. I'm also hoping that involving him in the investigation will help us keep tabs on the information and prevent any pertinent details… well… going astray, for want of a better term."

Dr. Clarke sat back, apparently appeased by Philip's reassurances. He looked at his watch.

"When does the meeting begin?"

Philip consulted the video recorder's clock.

"Seven fifteen. But I did have plans to be there a little early and speak with the witnesses first."

Dr. Clarke slowly nodded his understanding.

"That's fine with me. I can drive around for a while until my cue comes along, if you understand my meaning."

Philip reached into his own briefcase and brought out a brown manila file, which he handed to Dr. Clarke.

"This is a brief summary of the case so far along with details of the witnesses and, most importantly, a map of the journey which they made on the twenty third, indicating where they encountered the bank of mist. If you follow this, you should have no difficulty whatsoever in finding their house."

Dr. Clarke scrutinised the map for a moment before leaning forwards and placing it on the table with a finger resting on the point where the Morrison's had encountered the mist.

"I don't know the area very well, but isn't this an unlit road?"

Philip nodded.

"You can say that again. When I was younger I used to meet up with a friend of mine and we'd race cars up and down there all night. There are some sections of that road which still scare the living daylights out of me."

The psychologist grinned at he pictured the two men pitting their finely-tuned cars against each other with boyish enthusiasm and complete abandonment of common sense. He indicated the sections of road immediately before and after the point which Philip had indicated.

"These areas look pretty lonely to me as well."

Philip agreed once again.

"You break down out there and you've got a hell of a long walk to the nearest phone, believe me."

Dr. Clarke pursed his lips in momentary consideration.

"I think I'll kill some time by going to take a quick look at this road before I meet up with you again."

Philip closed his briefcase.

"Okay, then. I've got to get moving now. Don't forget, Henry, seven fifteen."

He raised a hand.

"I'll be there. What about the reporter?"

"I've asked him to come along at seven fifteen as well. He has directions to the house, but he hasn't got a case file yet."

Dr. Clarke nodded approvingly.

"Probably a wise move."

Pamela started as Alan touched her gently on the shoulder. She realised, with surprise that she had been standing for some time with both hands immersed in a bowl of dirty washing up water.

"You awake, Pam?"

She removed her hands and began to dry them.

"Only just. I feel like I've got 'flu or something coming on."

"I don't feel so good myself. Come into the living room and get yourself warm. It won't be long before Philip gets here with his friends."

She followed him into the room and pulled her armchair up to the fire. Rain continued to batter against the window panes and the temperature was dropping sharply as darkness closed in prematurely on the rugged landscape. She rubbed life back into her hands and shivered, more at the approaching night rather than the cold. Alan moved a little closer to her and took her hand in his. He was surprised at how cold she was and he immediately reached out and turned the fire up. Its warming glow became a glowing blaze and they both moved as close as they dared. He saw the worry in her eyes and placed a comforting hand on her knee.

"Don't worry, love. Whatever happens it will all turn out for the best. We did the right thing by letting Philip bring his friends in. I'm sure the psychologist will know what to do."

She smiled weakly.

"I hope so, Alan. I can't take much more of this."

They both turned at the now-familiar roar of Bellamy's Triumph as he drove slowly up the cul-de-sac. The engine stuttered into silence and there was a knock on the door a moment later. Alan ushered the investigator into the room and Pamela stood unsteadily to greet him. He shook the rain from his hair and warmed himself by the fire for a moment.

"Hell of a change in weather, eh?"

Pamela shivered again.

"Thank God someone else is cold as well. I was beginning to think I was getting sick."

Concern darkened Philip's face as he straightened up and looked at both of them.

"How are you both?"

Alan spoke first.

"We've not been getting a lot of sleep because of the nightmares, but, apart from that, I don't think we're doing too badly."

"Has anything else come out other than what you told me about yesterday?"

Alan stood and began to draw the curtains as he spoke.

"I think everything is becoming more and more confused with each dream that I have. We've not spoken much about the dreams themselves, so I don't know what it's been like for Pamela."

Philip turned to her with a questioning look on his face. She began to speak hesitantly, but was almost immediately reassured by the investigator's warm and sympathetic approach.

"I think my dreams have been much the same as Alan's, but I haven't been getting as confused. Everything's still as clear as it was on Friday night."

Alan switched the room lights on.

"I was just about to make a brew when you came. Do you want tea of coffee, Philip?"

He sat on the sofa at Pamela's invitation and opened his briefcase.

"I'll have tea, if that's okay with the both of you. Do you mind if I tape record this session?"

Alan caught Pamela's eyes and voiced their mutual worry.

"We don't mind about that, but we're still both a bit worried about you involving that reporter. If this gets out, we could be finished around here."

Philip spread his hands in reassurance.

"I understand how you must feel, but you mustn't worry. I've involved Howarth for two reasons. Firstly, he's a member of the local group and he has some experience in this field, so his presence may be of use to all of us. Secondly, it will be a great deal easier to keep the story quiet if we involve him and constantly stress the importance of confidentiality. I know that if he were to find out about this tomorrow, without realising the gravity of the situation, he would go ahead and run an alien kidnap story and then the you-know-what would really hit the fan."

Alan seemed reassured by this. Pamela's face held a question.

"You speak like this has happened before, Philip?"

"This is the case. There are many people who have undergone similar experiences and have lived to tell the tale. I don't want to go into these yet, if you don't mind, because I think that each case must be dealt with in isolation for a short while. However, people from all walks of life such as a housewife, a policeman, a joiner and a retired naval officer have all been through something similar to what you are experiencing now. I believe that Dr. Clarke worked with the naval officer I have just mentioned."

Philip noticed a strange suppressed curiosity within Alan. It was as if he had questions, but asking them would be tantamount to accepting the events of the past few days. It was Pamela who spoke again.

"What has become of these people?"

"They are all still healthy and alive. Each one has dealt with the experience in a different way, but all have coped."

He looked expectantly at Alan and saw a question form in his mind, but his lips were still when a knock sounded at the door. Pamela laid a hand on his arm as he moved towards the kitchen door.

"You stay where you are, I'll get it."

She left and returned a few moments later accompanied by Dr. Clarke and Andrew Howarth. They both took the seats towards which she gestured and gratefully accepted the offer of a drink. Alan noticed that the psychologist was preoccupied with studying the room's décor closely and was playing little attention to the papers which rested on his knee. He caught Dr. Clarke's quick eye for a moment and saw a sharp brightness edged with a kindly glint which Alan rarely saw. He found himself returning the psychologist's warm smile and he stood to shake hands with him. The man's grip was firm and reassuring.

"I must complement you on your tastes, Mr. Morrison."

Alan looked at the room's décor and waved a dismissive hand at it.

"Most of this was Pamela's work. She chose it. I just hung it."

Alan knew that he was being evaluated and didn't feel uncomfortable when he faced the psychologist's subtly analytical gaze.

"Nevertheless, your tastes as a couple are impeccable."

Pamela returned with a tray full of mugs and they all took their seats. Philip began to speak.

"Firstly, I want to thank you all for coming here tonight and I would especially like to thank Alan and Pamela for allowing us to invade their privacy at such short notice. I don't know just how Dr. Clarke intends to do things, so I'll leave you in his capable hands. Feel free to ask questions at any time, but don't be put off by me being here."

He looked to Dr. Clarke, who began to speak in his clipped, well-modulated tones.

"To start with, I would also like to thank you all for your co-operation in allowing this meeting to take place. I am sure I speak for everyone when I say that we will do all we can to help you. As Philip has no doubt told you, I am a psychologist. I have been practicing since 1965 and have treated all forms of psychological disorders, but I hasten to add that I shall not be treating this case as such. I dealt with a person some years ago who had experienced something similar to that which you report now and I must confess I made many mistakes then. I hope that I have learnt from them, but I'll understand if, at any time in the future, you feel as if you are getting in too deep and wish for the investigation to be stopped."

There was a brief silence before Andrew Howarth began to speak without invitation.

"I'll just butt in here and tell you a bit about myself. I think you're a bit worried because I'm a reporter and all of that, but I promise you that none of this will make it as far as the papers unless you want it to, so you needn't worry. You no doubt know by now that I edit the local paper and that I also have contacts with the larger papers. I've been reading a bit about this abduction business and I have to say that I'm very interested."

Rain continued to beat against the windows as silence once again settled on the room. Dr. Clarke took out a notepad and pen.

"If you are both feeling up to it, I'd like to ask you a few questions now."

Both Alan and Pamela gave their consent to this. Dr. Clarke sat back slightly and opened the area between them. He looked at Alan who also relaxed at little.

"Okay, Alan. I'd like you to begin by telling me about your experiences of the last few days. Philip has given me some details of the interview he conducted already, but I'd like to hear your version, if you don't mind."

The psychologist sat back further and leant his chin on the thumb and index finger of his right hand. He listened carefully as Alan recounted the encounter with the fog, the missing time and the subsequent nightmares and upsets. Philip followed Alan's account and was surprised to find no major inconsistencies with the transcript of Sunday morning's interview. He noted this down and flashed the message at Dr. Clarke during a moment when neither Alan nor Pamela was looking their way. He nodded once, the movement almost imperceptible and quickly assumed his attentive posture as Alan turned to him upon conclusion of his story. He nodded before turning to Pamela.

"Okay, Pamela. You must have realised by now that I don't bite, neither do I laugh or joke. With this in mind, would you like to tell me about your experiences over the last few days?"

She began to speak with more hesitancy than Alan. Had the psychologist known about yesterday's visit to her parents, then he would have realised that Pamela had become very unwilling to relate her version of events as a result of the ridicule she had received.

"I was getting a bit worried because Alan was speeding to get home in time for the snooker which Dad had said he would tape anyway. I was just about to say something to him when Wendy, that's our daughter, by the way, shouted and drew our attention to a shooting star which was falling towards the hills to our left. We watched it for a moment before it disappeared. The next thing was we turned the corner and Alan banged the brakes on harder than I would have thought possible. I nearly cracked my head on the dashboard . When I straightened up there was a green mist in front of us. Well, I say mist, but it was thicker than that, more like smog of some kind. Anyway, I was scared daft, but Alan pressed on."

She paused and took a deep swallow of tea.

"Wendy screamed then and said that she'd seen a face at the window. I got a bit worried, in case there were some animals on the road and we'd driven straight into one. Next thing was we were out of the mist and on the way home. I couldn't understand how we had got through it so quickly, because it appeared really thick. I could only think that it had disappeared as we had been driving through it."

She looked to Dr. Clarke.

"You want me to go on?"

He indicated indifference with his remaining hand and smiled comfortingly.

"Only if you want to, Pamela."

"Okay, if it's going to be of some use to you. We got home and Alan collared me as soon as I'd got my coat off and pointed at the video clock. The damned thing was out again and I though there had been a power cut at first until he showed me all the rest of the clocks. They were all wrong by about three hours. I didn't get worried. In my job, you can't afford to crack at every little thing. I thought, then, about the sheep we might have hit. There was a hell of a bump just after we got out of the mist, you see. I phoned the police to check if there had been any reports of farm animals wandering about in the roads, but they didn't know of any. I checked the time with the desk officer and he confirmed what our clocks said. I was too buggered to think about it then, so we both went to bed. I don't know what time I woke up, but I remember that Alan was shaking me. I'd had a hell of a dream."

Silence fell for a moment as she looked to Alan for support. He took hold of her hands reassuringly. Dr. Clarke gestured for her to continue when she felt ready. When she began to speak again, the unsteadiness in her voice gave an inkling of the fear which the memories of her dream held for her.

"We were inside this bright white room and I was taking my clothes off. I don't know why, I just was. There were these small things all around, about this big thing."

She used her hand to indicate a height around four feet from the floor in front of her.

"They were all around Wendy. There were two larger men standing by, it looked like they were supervising or something like that. Then one of them stepped forwards and I got a good look at him. He wasn't like the smaller ones; in fact, he was almost human with the exception of his eyes, which were like a cat's. He produced a thing a bit like a penknife and placed it over Wendy's abdomen. At this point, I just thought that they were going to kill us all and I wished that Alan was there. I couldn't understand why Wendy wasn't fighting back and I remember I just began yelling at them to leave her alone. I just couldn't stand seeing my kid lying there."

Tears welled up in her eyes for a moment, but she wiped them away with the heel of her hand and continued with dogged determination.

"Alan must have woken me up at this point because I remember I was still screaming when I opened my eyes. I just couldn't stand them touching her at all. The funny thing about this dream was that it was all in a kind of slow motion, as if something had slowed my entire psyche down to a crawl. I think Alan had come from the bathroom because his face was still wet. I could see in his eyes that he was still scared as well. I didn't need to ask him why because I knew, somehow, that he had had the same dream. We were both too shocked to talk about all of this, so we just lay there. We must have drifted off back to sleep again, because the next thing I knew, I was back in that damned room again. I almost couldn't believe it when one of the larger things took a device shaped like a needle and stuck it in me. I thought it would hurt like hell, but I couldn't feel a thing and it was then that I became aware of a hand over my forehead. I heard this weird voice then. Well, I say 'heard', because that's the only word I know to describe it. It was like the words were already there, it was strange. I somehow knew that Wendy and Alan were going to be okay and that we wouldn't be harmed. I noticed then that all the men were stepping away and then a large light passed over my body. It was like a big, moving fluorescent light, only much brighter. When that snapped off, I was in another room with Alan and Wendy and I was dressed again."

She paused again and took a breath to steady herself. Alan squeezed her hand comfortingly.

"I was bloody glad to see them again, I'll tell you that. There was a kind of screen on the wall of this room which we were in. This began to fill with images and it felt like I was surrounded by it after a moment. All I could see were pictures of polluted water grounds, wars, riots, things like that. It all went too fast for me to take in, but I could feel that there was an incredible sense of loss in all of these images. The only way I can describe it is by using that 'smellyvision' as an example. Can you remember the days when we used to get those cards at the cinema and we were told to scratch and sniff them at a certain point in the film to give it a bit more realism? It was the same here, only there were feelings associated with each image: fear, pain, hunger, misery.

"All the lights went out and then we were back on the road. There was a terrific bump and then the car rolled out of this mist. It was then that I realised that this dream had not been in slow motion like the last one. It all felt too real this time. I had much the same dream on Saturday night and I haven't been able to sleep properly since then."

It seemed at that point that her body understood the story to be finished. She released the hold she had on Alan's hand and slowly sank back into the chair as if her vitality had been suddenly drained.

Philip shot a look at Howarth and noted he was scribbling intently. Dr. Clarke hadn't moved since he sat down nor had he made more than half a page of notes. He checked his tape recorder and sat back once more. Dr. Clarke drew a line across the page of his notepad and scribbled a new title before looking up at them both again.

"I hope you don't mind me asking the next question, but I am afraid that it is an important one. Can we start with you, Alan? Were you touched in a sexual way whilst you were on board?"

Alan shook his head.

"Not that I can remember, unless you want to call the bit with the wire sexual."

Dr. Clarke shook his head.

"No, I mean outside of the actual examinations you have just described."

He angled his body to face Pamela.

"How about you, Pamela? Can you remember being touched at all?"

She fingered her empty teacup for a moment and looked down at the carpet as a wave of embarrassment swept over her.

"Well, yes, I was. I think I was examined internally and I can also remember feeling my breasts being touched, but it felt like they were being touched out of curiosity rather than any other purpose."

The doctor nodded and turned back once more to address the both of them.

"I am sure that this is a question which Philip asked you both, but I hope you won't mind answering it again for me. Could you tell me about your relationship over the last couple of months, any problems which you may have had or anything like that?"

Alan spoke first.

"I think we've always had a good relationship. I know that we understand each other and that helps us ride out the rough times when they come along. We've both been very busy over the past few months and I think we've drifted apart as a result of that. I hope it isn't permanent, though."

Pamela smiled at him, taking hold of one of his hands and squeezing it comfortingly.

"I think Alan speaks for me as well there. I've noticed that we've been drifting apart as well and I've felt responsible for this in a way. You see, when I have a hard time at work, I come home and I tend to give Alan a hard time as well. I've also been very introspective lately and I haven't been saying much to him. I had been planning to make it up to him over the weekend, but I never got the chance with all of this."

The psychologist nodded with understanding.

"Finally, then, I'd like to just go back into your past for a moment. It helps my understanding of cases like this if I can relate a similar experience to anything which may have gone on in your respective pasts. Have either of you ever had any form of paranormal experience of any kind?"

Pamela straightened up in her chair quickly as if charged with energy once again.

"You're not kidding. Me and Janice, that's a colleague of mine at work, we have this ongoing joke because every time she rings me up, I know it's her before I pick the receiver up. It's funny, I've known things have been going to happen before. There was a time when Wendy fell over and cut her arm very badly. All I could think about for hours before was ringing the hospital for some reason and I kept feeling the need to cut plasters off the roll. I thought it was really strange at the time, but later on, it all made sense.

"I can also remember seeing two old people in my mum and dad's bedroom. I shouted at them to get out, because I thought they were going to rob the place and when I looked back, they were gone. My mum and dad came running upstairs, wondering what all the noise was about. I described the two people and my dad sat down heavily on one of the stairs. I later found out that he was shocked because I had just described his mum and dad as they were when they died together in bed before I was born."

Alan took Pamela's silence as his cue to speak.

"I knew about these experiences because Pamela has told me before. I've not experienced anything at all myself, with the exception of one case when I was very young. I can remember waking up and seeing this shape hanging over my bed which looked for all the world like my grandfather. He died long before I was born and I'd only seen him in old photographs, so I never was sure just what I saw then."

Dr. Clarke closed his notebook just as Alan finished speaking. He smiled warmly again.

"I'd like to thank you both for being honest with me and for giving me your time. I'd like now to go and study the notes that I have made and also to consider carefully what you have said. However, I should like to take things a step further if you are in agreement."

Alan and Pamela both looked at him in anticipation and accepted the papers which he passed to them.

"Hypnotic regression is a process which has been used in the medical profession for some time now to help amnesia victims recover their lost or disjointed

memories over a period of time. It hasn't got anything to do with all that rubbish you seen on the television where these people have members of the audience floating all over the stage. I was just hoping that employing this may help reduce in magnitude and eventually eradicate the problems which you have had since the experience itself. What I've given you there are photocopies from various trade journals arguing the pros and cons of regression. If you wish you can read them and make up your own minds. Above all, remember that what I make here is only a tentative suggestion, the choice is yours."

Alan scanned the articles thoughtfully for a moment before looking up at the psychologist.

"Have you used this kind of thing before?"

"I've used hypnotic regression to help the witness I spoke to you about earlier. This allowed the witness to be freed of the nightmares which he was experiencing and were similar to the ones you report and it also allowed the full abduction experience to become clear during the course of the session. I usually find that in these cases the story rarely changes, but the relaxed state of the witness allows a much more exact recall of the events."

Pamela's enthusiasm was obvious, but Alan still remained reserved. Dr. Clarke looked at them both.

"The choice is yours; I won't hurry you into making a decision. Now, I believe Philip has a couple of questions to ask you."

The investigator looked up from his notes.

"Yes, nothing important, I just wanted to ask either of you if you've ever read any UFO literature of any sort: books, magazines, that kind of thing."

They looked at each other for a moment before Pamela turned and grinned.

"We took Wendy to see *ET* a couple of years ago, but that's about it."

Philip made a quick tick on his notepad before looking up with a bright smile on his face.

"Okay, that's my curiosity satisfied. I think we can call it a day, unless Mr. Howarth has any questions."

The reporter shook his head almost absentmindedly, not looking up from his own notes which he was studying with an almost childlike obsession. The psychologist stood to leave, smiling comfortingly at Alan and Pamela.

"Thank you, both of you, for your co-operation. I hope it's not been too difficult for you. I'm not trying to force anything on you here, but I do feel the regressive therapy would be of a great help here. Since I would be doing this outside of my official capacity, there would be no charge, of course."

Alan shook his proffered hand and showed him to the door. Howarth stood and followed him, ignoring Pamela's goodbyes and speaking to Philip in hushed tones. Once on the drive, they parted company, Howarth to his Volvo, Henry Clarke to an Austin Maestro and Philip Bellamy to his beloved Triumph. Its roar drowned out the subdued whines of the other two vehicles as they left. As Alan busied himself making tea, Pamela scanned over the articles which the psychologist had left. She raised her voice in order that it would carry through to Alan in the kitchen.

"What do you think of this regression hypnosis, Alan?"

He walked slowly into the living room and set two cups of tea carefully down onto the table before answering.

"I don't know, Pam. All of this is getting stranger by the minute."

She laid the papers on the arm of her chair and turned to face him as he sat down.

"Think about the last couple of days, Alan. Unless something is done, I've got this feeling that things are just going to get stranger."

She could see a grudging agreement dawning on his tired features. Seeing the advantage, she pressed her point home with determination.

"Look, we'll both go mad if we don't get a good night's sleep. I got the impression that this is a course of treatment. If neither of us like the first session, then there's nothing stopping us from bottling out. What do you think?"

Alan took a brief look at the articles, too briefly for their contents alone to form his decision.

"Go ahead and phone the guy if you want. It can't do any harm, can it?"

As she lifted the receiver in the kitchen and began to dial, she hoped that he was right.

******

PART FOUR

BETRAYAL

CHAPTER TWELVE

PARALLELS

The next morning brought a wintry sun, which rose slowly over the masses of grey clouds and shone weakly on the bleak landscape. Little more than an hour after dawn, the clouds gathered further and began throwing their cold and damp assault at the hills and valleys.

The day dragged for both Alan and Pamela. They both felt as if they were changing, taking on a new mental form which alienated them from their colleagues. Both struggled for an understanding which eluded them. They longed for the day to end and yet feared what the evening session with Henry Clarke may reveal.

As his day ended, Alan drove Wendy over to Julie's house before collecting a takeaway meal and meeting Pamela who was leaving the office early. They both poked at their food without enthusiasm and left the house long before their seven thirty appointment with the psychologist was due.

Alan again followed the route which avoided the road where they had first encountered the mist. He made the detour without comment, feeling that he was ensuring their own safety and also worrying that he was giving in to a deeper urge to avoid that place.

Pamela's tired mind continued to spin almost autonomously, mixing new ideas and existing concerns and worries, forcing her once more to consider their strange encounter. Had she been subjected to some bizarre form of cosmic kidnap and rape? Had she merely been a casual plaything or was there significance to the events which now dominated her life and threatened to destroy her totally at any time?

She thought back over the past few months. Sexual frustration had led to a bizarre rape fantasy which had followed her through her dreams, but she had created that herself as a form of fulfilment, never imagining she would be subjected to such a thing in the real world. She felt lost and alone despite Alan's comforting presence. There was a burning desire to be loved within her which only she was capable of feeling.

Before her mind could wander elsewhere, her train of thought was broken by Alan's voice.

"Looks like this is it."

She looked up and saw a modest detached bungalow set in its own grounds, a discreet distance away from its identical neighbours. Alan manoeuvred the car into the drive and they looked at each other for a moment before leaving the car's protective bulk. He knocked on the hardwood door and attempted to calm his jumping nerves as he heard movement in the hall beyond.

The door was opened by Dr. Clarke. He wore the same loose-fitting casual clothes, but seemed more at ease in his home surroundings than he had been at their house yesterday. He ushered them into a large and tastefully decorated living room where Andrew Howarth and Philip Bellamy were busying themselves with assembling a video camera. The investigator looked up and smiled at them as they entered.

"I hope you don't mind any of this. Henry feels that watching a video recording of the session may help you understand better what you will say under hypnosis. We wanted to get it done before you got here. Sorry about the mess and fuss."

The psychologist returned with two steaming mugs of tea and handed them one each.

"I hope you won't object to this. We can do the session without any form of recording if you wish, but the therapeutic value of hypnosis can be doubled if the person in question can see his or her own sessions when they are out of the hypnotic trance. I am hoping that this will help you to integrate whatever memories emerge into your conscious recollection of events." He smiled. "It also beats having to read my notes as well."

They exchanged glances before Alan spoke.

"I don't think we'll mind, as long as the videotape stays with you, Henry."

The psychologist spread his hands in a gesture of reassurance.

"Of course. I wouldn't dream of having anyone outside of this room see the recording. Of that, you can be assured."

Alan nodded and shot another quick glance at Pamela.

"Let's get on with it then."

He led them from the living room through the hall and into a study at its end. The room was spacious and minimally furnished with a triangular arrangement of three chairs in its farthest corner. Ceiling-mounted spot lamps had been set to shine softly on the wall above. He gestured to the two chairs with their backs to the wall before taking the third which faced them both. He pulled a small writing table a little closer to the arm of the chair and flipped a notepad open.

"Firstly, I want both of you to relax while I tell you a little more about what the process of hypnosis entails. You won't be sailing off to any fantasy worlds and neither will I be forcing upon you a form of truth drug. You will both be in a state of extreme relaxation and this will hopefully allow any suppressed memories to surface in your conscious minds. I am hoping that this process will remove the amnesia from which you both seem to be suffering. There is quite a good chance that there won't be a great deal of success this time, but I am hoping that there will be some progress after a couple of similar sessions. You can both help me by relaxing as much as you possibly can and by making yourselves amenable to the suggestions which I will make during the session. If I think that there is any danger at all to either of you, then I will take you out of the trance immediately. Do either of you have any questions?"

They both sat in a numb silence. After a pause the psychologist began speaking in a quieter voice. They both felt tensions begin to slip away and their bodies relaxed almost involuntarily as if their reserves of energy were finally exhausted. After some time their pallor was waxy and solid, their mouths hung slightly open and their bodies were slumped in the chairs. Dr. Clarke left his seat to quietly open the door and admit Bellamy and Howarth, who quickly started the mini-cam and seated themselves on the floor by its tripod. He retuned to Alan and Pamela and began to speak.

"You are now in a very deep sleep. You are travelling back in time to that Friday night. I want you both to imagine a clock which is going backwards faster and faster. Soon you will reach the time when you are about to begin the journey and then you will both raise the index fingers of your right hands to tell me that you are there."

A heavy silence descended upon the room for a number of minutes before both raised their fingers almost simultaneously.

"Good. Now, Pamela, I will tap you on the head and you will hear nothing more until I do so again."

He reached out and tapped her lightly on the right temple. Immediately, her finger dropped back onto the chair's arm and her head slumped slightly. He turned to Alan.

"Where are you now, Alan?"

"I'm driving through the village and joining the main road."

"Where have you just been?"

"We've just been to visit Pamela's mum and dad."

"Did you enjoy the visit, Alan?"

"It wasn't too bad really. Albert sometimes takes some dealing with, but he was okay tonight. He actually gave me and Pam a bottle of wine. He also said he'd tape the snooker match for me. I don't think he's as bad as I sometimes remember him."

"Could I say everything went well for you then, Alan?"

Alan paused before answering.

"I was hoping that I could patch things up with Pam, but she doesn't seem to be interested. I had a few words with Valerie, but even she can't help me now. I was hoping that she could offer some advice."

"At what time did you leave Pam's parents house, Alan?"

He paused again for thought.

"It must have been about nine thirty-five. I checked my watch just before we left, because I wanted to see the snooker, even though Albert was taping it for me. I've followed this tournament."

"Did you watch the snooker, Alan?"

Silence fell again. Alan's features, immobile up until this time, suddenly registered a feeling of obvious unease. He began to speak more quickly.

"No. I missed the match."

"What time did you arrive home, Alan?"

"It was some time after 1am."

"So it took you nearly three hours to make a journey which should only take about thirty minutes?"

Alan's unease became more apparent. His fingers began to tighten their grip on the chair's arms.

"We broke down on the way home."

"Go on, Alan."

"We're going through the junction and taking the main road. I wanted to get home to watch the match and I had my foot down. Pam doesn't like it, but it was okay, there was nothing else on the road. Pam's chatting to Wendy and looking at the speedometer, but she doesn't say anything to me until we come to this bend. Then she tells me to watch it. I'm pulling into the bend. Bloody hell!"

"What is it, Alan?"

"Bloody mist in the middle of the road. I slam on the brakes and Pam nearly hits the dashboard. It's the oddest mist I've ever seen. The headlamp beams just bounce back off, even on full beam, and it doesn't seem to be swirling or anything. I hope it's not some poison or anything. I check that all the windows are up before setting off slowly and driving in to it."

"Do you break down now, Alan?"

His unease grew into a state of discomfort as the memories flooded back unhindered.

"Yes. I want to wake up now. Please wake me up."

"Steady, Alan. Don't forget where you are. You can tell me everything that took place without causing an outcry. Just carry on now."

He relaxed and his hands released their hold on the chair arms.

"We go into the mist and then Wendy screams out from the back seat that there's a face in the window. I know it can't be a face, but I start to get worried. If something's got out of one of the fields and I hit it in this mist, then we could be in some real trouble. Broken down in the middle of nowhere in this mist. It's bloody spooky. Then..."

"Go on, Alan."

"The bloody car just stops. It doesn't splutter, it just stops dead. The radio was on, but now all of its lights have gone out and there's just a soft hiss coming from the speakers, like what you get in between two tracks on the tape. I can hear this noise now. A sort of grating noise which gets louder. It's like a dentist's drill, going right through you. I look across at Pam and she's got a frightened look on her face. Wendy's crying and shying away from the windows like there's something out there. Poor kid – it looks like she's scared daft."

"What happens next, Alan?"

"The bloody car's vibrating now. It's like there's some heavy machinery somewhere around. There's a light in the mist as well. Great! Something's coming the other way and I haven't got a flying clue what side of the road I'm on."

"Can you hear the car engine noise Alan?"

"That's weird.

"Carry on, Alan. What's weird?"

"There's a light, but there's no sound... Bloody hell!"

"What's happening, Alan?"

"There's a big ball of light in the mist. It's shining red and green and it's getting closer."

"Has something caught fire, Alan? Are you all okay?"

"Yeah, we're okay, but this is getting weird. Oh... oh shit. I want to wake up now."

"Remain calm, Alan. Remember where you are. Nothing can harm you. Just continue with your story and stay calm and relaxed."

"There are three of them. Three of them silhouetted in front of the ball of light. They're looking at me and Pam now. Their eyes are burning into the back of my skull. Hang on a minute. Now the doors are open and they're taking Pam."

Alan began to scream in terror.

"Bring her back, you bastards! Christ we're all going to die now! Fucking hell! They've taken her into the light!"

"Calm down, Alan. You can tell me everything without disturbing me. There's no need to shout at all. Just tell me what's going on."

"Wendy's gone as well now. There's only one of them left in front of the lights. He's taller than the other two. About my height and his head's really weird. It's almost as if it's out of proportion with the rest of his body. He looks like he wants feeding up as well. He's a really spindly bloke. He's saying something to me."

"Do you hear him, Alan? Is he shouting?"

"Not shouting. He's not really saying anything. It's just like the words are in my head. They're getting louder and clearer all the time. He's telling me to come with him. He's saying 'don't be afraid'. That's bloody stupid because I'm scared shitless. He's coming closer now and I'm floating."

"Are you floating, Alan? Is it just how you are feeling?"

"I just feel that way. I've got my eyes closed now. I don't know where I am. I'm not going to open them in a hurry either. I can't stand them looking at me. They're there, though. Little bastards seem to be talking about me. God, I don't want them to hurt me. Where are Pam and Wendy?"

"Do they say why they have confronted you, Alan? Why have they stopped you?"

"They're not saying anything about that. I can't understand what they're saying, but this tall guy just keeps telling me not to be afraid."

"I want you to open your eyes and tell me where you are, Alan. Don't be afraid of what you'll see. Open your eyes and stay calm and relaxed. Are you in the car?"

"I'm... I'm not in the car anymore."

"Have these men taken you to their car, Alan?"

"Well... yeah. It's not a car though. I'm floating and I feel really funny. I'm not walking, but I'm moving. I don't want to go, but I don't really have any objections. It's all unclear, but there's a lot of bright light here and it's very white."

"Carry on, Alan. Are you in a room?"

"Yeah, it's a room and I'm lying on a couch or something like it. I'm trying to look around, but I can't move my head too far. It's just all light. Really bright white light and its cold. Oh, Christ. I feel like I'm a piece of meat just being saved for later!"

"Stay calm and relaxed, Alan. Can you still see these men? Can you tell me what they're doing?"

"They're trying to calm me down. One of them is messing about with tubing around my head and the other is fixing me with those black eyes. We won't be harmed. Pam and Wendy are okay. Now there's a pressure on my head and I can't even move that. They're shoving something in my ears and it hurts like hell. I scream out. Bloody hell it hurts. Like its going right through my head. Now it's all gone black and it's very quiet."

"Where are you now, Alan?"

"I don't know."

"What are you doing?"

"I... I'm not afraid anymore. Yes, it all makes sense now. We're going to be okay."

"What makes sense, Alan? I don't understand you."

"I can see images of new places. There are people dying. The place is black and dead, nothing lives and nothing moves. They're killing each other as well, but they don't want to harm us at all. It's so sad. They're ordinary people just like you and me. It's just the way they appear which sets them apart from us."

"Do you feel you have been robbed, Alan?"

"No, they're not here to rob."

"What else did they did they tell you, Alan?"

"I can't say."

"Why not? Did they threaten you?"

"I just can't tell you at the moment. I understand why they don't want me to tell you."

"What does this man look like? Take a close look at him and describe him for me."

"He's tall, at least six feet, and very human-looking. He has long blond hair. He's wearing this grey tight-fitting overall. His eyes are strange. They're like cat's eyes, slitty and dark. He's smiling and he's reassuring me."

"What do you see around you, Alan?"

"It's just a bright light. I think the walls are smooth and shiny as well."

"Is there any furniture of any sort?"

"I can see blocks which look like machinery. There's flashing lights on them and wires and tubing leading to and away from them. The things around them are disgusting."

"What are these things? What do they look like?"

"They're small like kids. They have elfish faces and dark eyes. They make weird high-pitched noises as they move around the room. The tall bloke seems to be in control of them."

"What happens now, Alan?"

"Bloody hell! My head's full of fire. The room is glowing brighter and brighter. Now it's getting hot. It's so hot that the green mist is disappearing. Now I can see the stars and the moon. Thank Christ for that! I thought we were going to hit something."

"Where are you now, Alan?"

"I'm in the car. Pam's okay and Wendy's asleep. They've gone home as well."

"Can you see the object now?"

"No. They've gone home.

"Okay, go on then."

"The radio comes back to life and the engine fires first time. The mist has gone and I can see where we're going again. Wendy's asleep in the back and Pam looks at me. She says 'I bet that one landed'. I don't believe in all the rubbish about UFOs. Time's getting on and I want to see the snooker. The car seems to be okay as we pull away."

"What time did you get home, Alan?"

"It must have been some time in the early hours. About one thirty, I think."

"How did you know the time?"

"Every clock in the whole place was showing the time."

"Didn't you think this was strange?"

"Maybe. I'm knackered. Eyes and head hurt like hell. I just want to get to bed. Forget the wine until tomorrow. It's okay 'because Albert's going to tape the snooker for me."

The psychologist sat back and closed his notepad. From the table beside him, he picked up another identical pad and recorded the time on its cover before opening it.

"Okay, Alan. I want you to go to sleep now. I don't want you to listen to anything else until I tap you on the head. You will hear nothing until I tell you to wake up."

He relaxed into the chair and his sweating began to subside. After a few moments, his grip on the chair's arms loosened and his body slumped. Dr. Clarke then tapped Pamela on the temple and went into a similar routine with her, in which he explored the events of the afternoon and the evening before their encounter. When they reached the beginning of the car journey he opened his pad and scribbled a brief note.

"What happens now, Pam?"

"We're driving back home. Alan is going like a bat out of hell. I don't think he can drive as well as he thinks he can. I'm worried about Wendy but I need a good night's sleep so I'm not bothered for myself. Wendy makes me jump when she screams something about a shooting star. I watch it as it passes over us and then I notice something strange about it. I've seen them before and this one just doesn't seem to fly like them."

"What do you mean by that?"

"It was strange, but I'm sure it passed in front of some trees on the hills on my right. I couldn't see any flashing lights on it, so it couldn't have been an aircraft."

"What happens after you see this light?"

"We come round a corner and I nearly fly through the sunroof as Alan slams on the brakes. In front of us, there's a bank of green mist. It's not like a fog, it doesn't swirl or drift. It just sits there."

"Go on."

"Alan and I are getting a bit worried by this. He winds his window up and turns to say something. Then Wendy screams. She's nearly hysterical and she's saying something about a face. My first thought is that there may be some animals loose from one of the fields. I don't want us to hit one. We're into the mist by now and suddenly the engine just cuts out and it takes the radio with it. Alan makes like he's going to take a look, but the torch in the glove compartment won't work, so he's stuck. Suddenly, there's this scraping noise inside my head. It hurts like hell. I get migraines, but this isn't one. It's just like something has hold of my head and its pushing from all sides. I know that Alan is experiencing the same thing. Then I can feel this heat on my face and there's pulsing red light in the mist. Now things begin to get frightening. We're immobile; we can't get out of here. Wendy looks okay – she's asleep, thank God."

For the first time in the session she became animated in the chair, lashing out with her arms as she screamed in terror.

"LEAVE ME ALONE! GET YOUR HANDS OFF ME! WENDY? WHERE ARE YOU? BRING HER BACK, YOU BASTARDS! THEY'VE TAKEN HER!"

"Calm down, Pamela. Relax and remain calm. You can't be hurt here. Just tell me what is going on."

"I'm not in the car anymore. There are hands all over me and we're being taken somewhere."

"Who's touching you? Are they hurting you?"

"There are these horrible little things, like dwarves. They're not hurting me, but they're dragging me into the light. Leave me alone! GO AWAY!"

"You're safe here. Tell me about the beings and this light."

"It's bright and red, pulsing, so it hurts my eyes at its brightest. They're touching me everywhere as they drag me along the road. Where's Wendy? Alan? Alan? Where the hell's Alan. Oh, Christ! We're going to die here."

"Remain calm, Pamela. Alan and Wendy are safe and you won't be hurt. Just tell me what happens next."

"It's just blank. Just black space."

"Where are you now?"

"I'm in a circular room. The small beings are all around me and one of them is attaching a device to my abdomen. It's stuck now and it hurts like hell. I try to ask what they're doing, but they don't seem to be able to understand me."

"What happens now?"

"There's this taller man here. He seems to be in control. He tells me that everything will be alright and the pain goes away just like that."

"How do you know he is in control? Does he tell you?"

"Yes. No... not really talks, it's just like the words are there. I feel safe now."

"Describe this man and the other beings for me, Pamela."

"He's human-looking, around six feet tall and he's wearing a kind of tight-fitting smock, a bit like a surgeon's. He's got long blond hair, almost feminine looking really!

Everything about him is okay, apart from his eyes. His eyes are black and oval, just like a cat's eyes. That's really weird."

"What about the other beings with you in the room?"

"They're short and they've all got long fingers. I can't see any facial features, just holes where mouths and noses should be. They all act in unison as they get hold of me. Oh, bloody hell!"

"Remain calm, Pamela. Just tell me everything without upsetting yourself."

"They're taking my clothes off now. It's like they say in those programmes about rape. Just submit and you won't get hurt. I don't want them to hurt me. One of the smaller ones has a thing like a knitting needle and he's bringing it closer to me."

She arched her back and began to tremble uncontrollably. The psychologist gradually calmed her down, describing images of well-being. After a while, she subtly returned to the story.

"Have you ever experienced pain like this before? Does this hurt for a long time?"

No, they prod and poke for a while before withdrawing it. Then there's this bright light which shines on me for a while before everything goes black. Oh, God, they hurt me. Why did they do this to me?"

"What happens now? Can you see what's going on?"

"I'm just lying there. It's cold and I'm shivering. The tall one is there, but the others have left me alone. I ask him why he's here and who he is. He just says that I'm not to know yet. If I try to find out, then harm will come to me. I don't want to be hurt again, so I shut up for a while. Then I ask him to at least tell me about himself. Everything goes quiet and I think I've done it. They're going to kill me, then... oh, Christ!"

"What happens, Pamela?"

"Another place, my head's dancing and exploding with pictures. It's feels like someone's tying my brain in knots. Fire and ice, a mushroom cloud, war, pollution and destruction. There's a blue-robed figure there, very much like the tall one who's here with me. There's sorrow and pain coming from him and then he gives me a message. So much killing, so much pain and torture. It hurts so much to see it. Decadence, drugs, violence, nobody to keep order and nobody to look after the sick."

"What about the message? What does he tell you?"

"I can't say?"

"Why not?"

"The time isn't right. I'll be hurt if I say now. They'll tell me when the time is right. They've left me alone now. It's all dark and I'm alone in the blackness. Where's Alan? Where's Wendy?"

"You're safe now. Just remain calm and relaxed. What do you do next?"

"I go back to the car. Wendy's safe and she's asleep. Thank God for that."

"Where is the blond man?"

"I can't see anybody now. It's just glowing and there's this green mist all around us."

"Where's Alan?"

"He's in the car with me, just looking at the glow."

"What does the glow look like?"

"No...wait! It's going away now. The vibration rises in tone – it doesn't hurt as much anymore. Now the glow changes from red to blue and then it fades out. Next thing is the mist just begins to disperse. Then I can see the stars through the sunroof and I know that it's all over. The car's engine is running again and it's lovely and warm. Alan turns round and looks at me. I say something about the mist making things look strange. I remember about flying saucers and remark about that to him. He just shrugs it off and then sets off home. The car's fine, picking up well."

"At what time do you arrive home, Pamela?"

"It was about half past one. Alan showed me the clocks, but I couldn't believe it at first, so I rang the police. They agreed with our clocks, so something big must have gone wrong. I don't know what, but it was strange, something to do with that thing on the road."

Dr. Clarke closed his pad and signalled to Bellamy and Howarth that the session was at an end. The investigator reached up and shut the power off to the video camera. The psychologist then turned back to Alan and Pamela and began to bring them out of their trances with constant suggestions of well-being and health. After some time, they were both aware of their surroundings and seemed disorientated, as if they had both awoken from a deep sleep. He made sure they could both hear him before he spoke.

"How do you both feel?"

Alan rubbed his eyes and tried to focus on the figure in front of him. As his body adjusted to the wakefulness, he remembered where he was. A broad smile began to spread across his face and this was complemented by a baffled look in his eyes.

"Okay. Good in fact. Ready for a drink."

Dr. Clarke nodded his satisfaction and turned to Pamela.

"You too?"

She stretched her cramped muscles as far as the confines of the chair would allow and smiled.

"Yeah. Shaking and... hungry. Starving in fact."

He returned her smile.

"Okay, you two just sit there for a while. Don't try to stand up yet or you'll fall over like a sack of potatoes. Wait until you can feel your legs before you try anything."

He turned to face Philip.

"Do you want to go and make some tea? You'll find biscuits and the like in the cupboard over the hob. Bring the lot in."

The investigator nodded.

"Okay. I could murder a brew myself."

Dr. Clarke turned back to Alan and Pamela as Philip left the room.

"Still okay? Do you feel up to watching your video after a cup of tea?"

They looked at each other uncertainly for a moment before Alan turned back to him.

"Okay. If Pam doesn't object, we might as well get it over with."

Dr. Clarke motioned to Howarth who extracted the tape from the video camera and left for the living room. Alan noticed a momentary look of worry pass over the psychologist's face as he looked back to him.

"Can either of you remember anything?"

Pamela looked at the ceiling for a moment before speaking.

"Yeah. It's a lot like my dreams, but it's all coherent now. I can remember the sequence in which things happened. I can see why we got home so late though! We must have been in that thing for hours. I don't think the periods of blackness were anything to do with the ship itself though. I think that I spent much of the time unconscious while they examined me. I don't know whether they meant it to happen or whether my own fear caused it."

Alan seemed to be experiencing more difficulty remembering his experiences. His face showed confusion and a dark preoccupation whilst Pamela's manner was calm and her attitude was one of acceptance. His voice seemed stressed.

"It seems like a dream to me. All those aliens and that great big light. Just like something out of *Close Encounters of the Third Kind.* Things like this just don't happen to normal people do they? I'm just wondering..."

A question froze on his lips and Dr. Clarke urged him to continue.

"I took a dose of LSD years ago at college and went on a bit of a bad trip. I've been worried about a flashback for ages. I thought that certain types of food or drink could cause it, even an extreme state of tiredness may bring one on. It feels a bit like one of them to be honest."

Before Pamela could respond to this, Philip walked back into the room with a laden tray balanced precariously on top of his case file. They all gratefully accepted a cup of tea and took them through to the living room at Dr. Clarke's request. Howarth, who had been eyeing the psychologist's chess trophies, looked up almost guiltily as they entered. He moved quickly to a seat and nodded to the video recorder beneath a large television set.

"It's all set up."

Dr. Clarke held the remote control unit and pressed a button which activated the TV receiver and the video recorder's circuits simultaneously. As the tape progressed through its playback, he occasionally glanced at Alan and Pamela who seemed entranced by the images of themselves under hypnosis. He noticed with satisfaction that Pamela's hand made frequent trips between her mouth and the biscuit barrel as a glow returned to her previously pale cheeks. Alan stared intently at the screen, but his hands slowly began to unlock as the story unfolded and soon he too relaxed into the sofa's comfortable folds. When the image finally flickered into a snowy nothingness, the doctor stopped the tape and switched the television off. Philip turned to Alan and Pamela.

"What do you think of that then?"

Pamela turned to him and he was amazed at the change. Her face had lost the deep lines it had held for the past week and her eyes caught and held his gaze with a steady, effortless confidence. Even her voice seemed calmer and more evenly modulated.

"That's a great weight off my shoulders anyway. I feel a bit like a person who has lived through a great disaster when everyone else hasn't made it. When we were stopped on the road and taken aboard that craft, I think I could have handled being able to remember it because no harm was really done. When they placed the block there, it meant that the memories could only emerge as bad dreams. Now that I know what has happened, I think I can cope with the memories. They weren't there to hurt us."

Howarth immediately cut in.

"Erm... this may seem a little forward, Pamela, but... could I have a look at the mark on your abdomen."

She grinned at his embarrassment.

"Of course."

She pulled her t-shirt free from the waistband of her jeans and lifted it until the small red mark above the buckle of her belt became visible. Howarth leant forward and inspected it closely for a moment before turning to Alan.

"What about the mark around your ear, Alan?"

He angled his head towards the reporter and parted his hair to reveal a similar mark just below and behind his ear lobe.

"It's faded a bit now, but it was really red on the Saturday morning."

"How do you feel about this, Alan?" asked Philip.

Once again Alan seemed at a loss for words.

"It's... well, it's strange. Bizarre might be a better word for it. If it wasn't for the marks, I wouldn't have accepted anything that came out during that session. It's got me baffled, but I feel better now that it's all out in the open."

Dr. Clarke seemed most pleased by this. He extracted the tape from the video machine and handed it to Pamela.

"This is for the both of you. I want you to watch it a number of times and then discuss what has come out during the session. Try not to become too embroiled in the whys and wherefores. Just carefully consider the available evidence and try to come to terms with what has taken place. This is probably the best way of integrating these memories fully into your conscious recall of that Friday night."

She took the tape with one hand and held onto his with her other.

"Thank you, Dr. Clarke. I don't think either of us could have taken anymore. You've done us a great favour. I just hope that an explanation can be found for this."

The psychologist smiled back and patted her hand gently.

"Think nothing of it, my dear. Now that all of this is out in the open, it's up to both of you to deal with it in your own way."

He sat back in his chair and addressed them all again.

"I'd like to conduct further sessions like this, if everyone is amenable. Further hypnosis will reinforce and build upon the foundations which have been laid down today."

Philip snapped his briefcase closed.

"I'll be keeping in close contact with Alan and Pamela until they are over the worst of this, so I'd be happy to work as the middle man."

Dr. Clarke nodded and looked to Alan and Pamela who were also in agreement with this.

"Okay, then. That seems to be about all that's worth doing for one night. Alan, Pamela, if either of you need anything at any time of the day or night, please don't hesitate to call me and I'll do what I can. I'll trust Philip to organise another session as I have other matters to attend to. I'm sure that you're in good hands with him, though."

The investigator nodded.

"You can count on it. I've already told you both that I'm available day and night. You've got my number. I'll give you a ring and call up as soon as it's convenient."

Both Alan and Pamela smiled as Dr. Clarke led them to the door. Philip looked across at Howarth who began scribbling furiously the moment the psychologist left the room. He also noticed that the tape recorder had been running for some time. He presumed correctly that the soundtrack of the entire session was held on the tape spool. He moved closer to Howarth and pointed.

"Did you record all of this?"

Howarth nodded without looking up from his pad.

"I'm building my own case file and I wanted a good recording of the hypnosis session. It's easier to transcribe the recoding this way."

Philip's eyes narrowed.

"I thought we agreed no story until we all decided to release it."

Howarth's head snapped up from the notebook. There was an irritated look on his face and there was something about his voice which made Philip nervous.

"Look. We made a deal, so let's forget about it now. I'll keep this story quiet until I get the go ahead."

He held Philip's gaze for a silent moment before looking beyond him to the door where Dr. Clarke was standing. Neither of them had been aware of his presence and they had no idea how much he had heard. He seemed untroubled and refrained from comment as he began to collect the empty teacups together.

"That was quite an interesting exercise for me, but it has left me a little tense. I was wondering if we might adjourn for a pint and talk over this evening's events."

Philip smiled as he recalled the smooth taste of the bitter served by The Rope and Anchor.

"How about a trip back to the village past the area where these events took place? Perhaps we can get a look at the site before it gets too dark."

Dr. Clarke seemed to approve of the idea and took Howarth's continued silence as agreement. He left the tray on a side table and stepped into the hall for a moment to retrieve their coats from ornate brass hooks.

"How do we get there, Philip?"

He smiled and lifted a hand to proudly display his Triumph key ring. Held in the psychologist's answering grin was a trace of child-like anticipation.

"I was wondering when I might get a ride in that fine machine of yours."

Philip looked proudly at the key ring.

"Yep! One hundred and forty miles per hour and seven years' worth of restoration. I'll give you both the ride of your lives!"

******

CHAPTER THIRTEEN

UNSATISFACTORY CONCLUSIONS

Darkness had fallen by the time they reached the small pub. The tolerable warmth of the day had remained and the air was clear and alive with the wild smells of the moorland. The calm of the village was disturbed only by a solitary, late evening chorus from a thrush, which floated gently over the freshly-ploughed fields. A welcoming yellow glow flooded over the threshold as they opened the door and went inside the tavern. They took up seats around the table in a corner booth and spent a few silent moments in relaxation until the drinks arrived. Philip took a mighty swallow of his bitter before turning to Dr. Clarke.

"Okay then Henry. You've spoken to the two witnesses and looked at the case in detail. I'd be interested in any opinions which you have now. Bear in mind that I shall be reluctant to discuss these with Alan and Pamela until we think they're ready."

He nodded and placed his beer carefully on the table before leaning back in his seat and speaking.

"Outside of my study of UFOs, I have only ever seen one case which parallels this. The patient in question, a middle-class young woman, was experiencing great difficulty in starting a family with her husband. She became understandably depressed as a result of her frequent miscarriages and was referred to me for treatment. During a number of sessions with her, it became apparent that she blamed herself for her inability to carry a child. Her husband tended not to get involved much with this and she felt that he also blamed her. Her inability to fulfil the basic needs within their marriage and within herself created a complex and it took me a number of months to find a successful treatment for this. The couple succeeded in having a child soon after this.

"While I was reviewing this woman's medical records some months later, her husband was also referred to me for treatment. He was suffering from fits of paranoia along with acute depression and he actually required hospitalisation for treatment. Looking back over *his* medical records, I was fascinated to discover a series of mild depression attacks which took place whilst his wife was seeing me, followed by frequent nausea and symptoms associated with water retention and hormonal imbalance."

He paused to take a mouthful of his lager.

"Before getting too deep into terminology, I'll tell you that the ultimate outcome of this was a diagnosis of a sympathetic pregnancy. There are a number of theories regarding this, but it does seem that a degree of non-verbal communication between husband and wife during the term of the pregnancy can trigger a series of physiological changes within the man's body. These can have symptoms very similar to those associated with the condition of pregnancy."

Howarth looked at his Coke for a moment in deep thought before taking advantage of Dr. Clarke's silence.

"Pardon me for asking, Henry, but how does this tie in with contact with aliens and flying saucers?"

This time, the psychologist did not disguise the pained look which he shot at Philip.

"I see this as a purely psychological event. The aliens and the flying saucer never had any reality outside of Pamela Morrison's mind."

Howarth laughed.

"Come on, Doc! I know that people can have wacky dreams, but don't you think you're pushing the grounds of credibility right off the edge of the world?"

Dr. Clarke smiled.

"Your reference to the flat earth concept is indeed interesting, Mr. Howarth. Perhaps that explains your limited insight into this. I suppose I had better abandon the parallels I was trying to draw and explain all of this from the beginning."

The reporter's silence was sullen as Dr. Clarke collected his thoughts.

"It seems to have begun soon after Pamela and Alan's daughter, Wendy, was born in 1978. There were various complications involved in the birth and this resulted in Pamela needing an emergency surgery to correct severe internal bleeding. It was also necessary for the surgeons to perform a hysterectomy at the time and, therefore, Pamela cannot bear any more children. It seems obvious to me that both badly want another child and this seems to be at the root of a curious, shared psychological complex which grew up between them and which the pressures of work have recently complicated. The clincher here was the preoccupation which the so-called aliens appeared to have with their sexual organs. Pamela's ordeal was not dissimilar to a typical rape scenario, so I think there is a degree of fantasy fulfilment here as well."

Howarth's voice was growing incredulous.

"But what about the missing time and the mist and the UFO? How come Alan was examined as well?"

"I was just on the point of moving on to that. Obviously the abduction is a bizarre experience which could only take place under certain conditions. The conditions were ideal on that night. An unlit road, two very tired people, one just stargazing, the other driving and watching the road. Here we have the ideal situation for a condition known as 'highway hypnosis' to take over in both cases. In this condition, a person can drive for hours on a form of 'automatic pilot' whilst the brain wanders elsewhere. This is very similar to a sleepwalking person. People under highway hypnosis have been known to negotiate complex intersections and to behave correctly at traffic lights and at other similar hazards. It is not unreasonable to assume that a culmination of circumstances brought about two separate cases of highway hypnosis here."

Dr. Clarke was about to continue, but Howarth chipped in quickly.

"But what about the aliens? Did they get them while they were hypnotised?"

The psychologist continued as if he hadn't heard him. Acknowledgment of his question would come later.

"When highway hypnosis takes over, the conscious thought processes of the mind are suspended until something out the ordinary occurs which will kick-start the conscious mind again. Something like returning home and noting a time lapse would be ideal. In this case, the lights of another vehicle on the road may well have woken Alan and Pamela up and then caused them to recall their experiences whilst they were entranced. They would have seen the receding lights and misinterpreted it as the craft of their dreams. In answer to your question Mr. Howarth, what actually takes place when the person is in the trance is even stranger.

"The doorways into the subconscious mind are opened. In this area of the mind, there is no concept of then and now, no time and no space. There are limitless dimensions and everything exists in a strange kind of 'now'. The subconscious also acts as a repository for the emotions, problems and feelings which the conscious mind cannot deal with for whatever reason. I am sure that both Alan and Pamela harboured

a great deal of guilt, fear, regret, anger and frustration within their own personal complexes and this all suddenly flooded out. The strange, dream-like abduction experience was the result."

"But where did the aliens come from?" Howarth framed his question carefully and spoke slowly and clearly. Dr. Clarke stiffened during its delivery and Philip saw his hand tighten on the neck of his glass.

"Within each of us is a vast library of archetypal images, some as old as the human race itself. The devil, the old man, the witch, the great warrior, the submissive woman. When Tolkien weaved his fantasy worlds with such delicacy and precision, he was taking a vast number of images from his own store to which we can all relate. As I have said, the operation of the subconscious mind is completely alien to our understanding. Emotions and feelings were woven into a strange dream filled with these archetypes. The benevolent alien, physically perfect and a symbol of the superhuman to which we all aspire, the spacecraft representing a high power and a degree of solace from earth-bound problems, the mischievous smaller animals placed as servants of the master. With Alan and Pamela, we have two highly intelligent and extremely aware people who are obviously concerned for the future of the world and for the life of their only child. Her deep-rooted fears about pollution, war and famine were also brought to the fore in the message given to her by her own mind."

Howarth goggled at this and turned to Philip, who was nodding his head.

"I couldn't agree more. Much of what you have said will be put in my conclusion when I write the case file up. I have one question though, Henry. Some people think that an alien power, even though not physically involved, may shape the imagery and thus send a message via the abduction experience. What do you think?"

The psychologist pursed his lips in thought for a moment before nodding slowly.

"One can never discount any of these possibilities. Certainly, there are many strange things which occur within the mind for which we have no real answer. In some cases, the theory of cause and effect does not hold water. What I have said is only a personal theory, but it does hold more water than the idea of a physical abduction. Even the marks can be explained in terms of stigmata phenomena. Religious devotees have died with imprints on their hands where Christ was crucified, even though no physical harm was done to them. I am sure this can happen to a greater or lesser degree during these abductions, which can also be seen as forms of a religious vision."

Howarth smiled to himself and quietly stopped the micro tape recorder in the pocket of his jacket. He finished his Coke and stood up, offering his hand to both of them.

"Well, I've got to get going now. I have a lot of work to do for that article in *The Dalesman* and I haven't even made a dent in it yet. I'll speak to you both soon."

He left without waiting for an acknowledgement. They looked at each other and Philip breathed a sigh of relief.

"Sorry about him, Henry. I'm sure he has a printing press going in his head at times. He's a good guy underneath all of that, but he likes things in black and white."

The psychologist stretched in the chair and placed his hands behind his neck.

"In my experience, there is no black and white, only varying shades of grey. It is a pity that the world's media works in many different forms of black and white. I also believe it is my round."

They both smiled and allowed the warmth and laughter of the pub to take them where it would.

Andrew Howarth shrugged change out his pocket as the telephone rang. He rammed a fifty pence piece into its slot as the receiver at the other end was lifted.

"Jennifer Lynton, please. Jennifer? Hi, it's Andrew Howarth here. You know that you said nothing ever happened up here? Yeah. Well, I've got something which will blow your doors off. Can you get round in, say, fifteen minutes?"

He replaced the receiver with a satisfied smile.

******

CHAPTER FOURTEEN

FRONT PAGE NEWS

Consciousness slowly seeped into Philip Bellamy's clouded brain. He slowly turned over in bed and winced at the light which poured through the window. He could hear a sound hovering on the periphery of his hearing, which was dulled by a throbbing headache. With a start, he realised that the telephone mounted on the wall above his bed was ringing shrilly. He groped for the receiver and clumsily unhooked it.

"Hello."

He snatched the receiver away from his ear as it grated with a shout from the other end.

"Who is this?"

"Have you read the bloody papers yet?"

He realised that the voice was Alan's. He slowly sat up in bed and fought the nausea which came over him.

"Alan? What the hell's up, mate?"

"What the fucking hell are you doing? We're all over the sodding *Daily World* this morning."

Wakefulness hit him like a sledgehammer and he was surprised at the incredulity in his own voice.

"You're what?"

Alan sounded as if he was on the edge of hysteria. He could hear Pamela sobbing in the background.

"We're splashed all over the centre pages of the paper! All the stuff about the case, photographs, fucking stupid drawings of UFOs and aliens, the bloody lot!"

"I haven't seen the paper yet."

Alan shouted so loudly that the receiver's speaker began to distort the signal.

"Well you can fuck off and get it then, can't you!"

Philip almost felt the force with which Alan slammed the telephone down, despite the fact that only a distant click actually signalled a broken connection. He shoved the covers aside and swung his legs over the side of the bed. He tried to recall the events of the previous night, but they hung tantalisingly out of his reach, suspended in a writhing sea of pain and discomfort. He tried to lick his parched lips, but his swollen tongue refused to move. With an almost superhuman effort, he lifted himself from the bed and staggered into the bathroom.

After ten minutes on his feet, the dizziness began to lift. He showered and dressed, ignoring the unmade bed for the moment and, instead, switching on the coffee maker in the kitchen. After a few minutes, there was a respectable pool of brown liquid in the bottom of the bowl, which he poured into a cup and used to wash four paracetamol down. The combination of tastes made him grimace and the bright morning stung his eyes and he emerged from the gloom of the staircase and the workshop.

Fighting disorientation, he headed towards the newsagent's and snatched a *Daily World* from the stand outside its door. He was already flicking through the paper as he paid for it. The middle page fell open on the counter and he stared in horror at what he saw.

THE GREEN MIST MARTIANS!

FAMILY SPACEKNAPPED

Surrounding the huge lettering were the pictures of the smiling Morrison family with small, stylised images of alien spacecrafts flitting around their margins. As he scanned the body of the article, he was bombarded with misquotes, distorted facts and ludicrous conclusions, obviously drawn by an individual conversant with the case, but ignorant of the nature of the family's experience. He realised that the woman behind the counter was looking worriedly at him.

"Are you okay, love?"

He folded the paper and used it to smack the palm of his right hand."

"No, and I know someone else who won't be in a while."

Within minutes, the village calm was shattered as Philip's Triumph roared down the main road. He doubled every limit he encountered as he sped towards Howarth's house on the moors beyond. As he reached the large bungalow, he brought the car to a screeching halt and left it with the engine running. He hammered on the house door until he heard the bolts inside being slowly drawn back. As the door swung back on its hinges, he bolted through the opening, grabbing Howarth by the neck as he did so. The reporter attempted to pull his arm away as Philip stuffed the newspaper into his fear-struck face.

"You little shit! Have you read your handiwork yet?"

Howarth croaked as he tried to draw air through his constricted windpipe.

"I never meant for it to be like this. I though they were going to do the story properly!"

Philip shoved the smaller man up against he wall.

"Properly? You sold a story to this rag and you wanted it doing properly? You dumb little shit!"

Howarth twisted away from his grip and attempted to escape from the hall. Philip caught him in one stride and put all his weight and anger behind the fist which he smashed into Howarth's terrified face. The reporter stumbled back before collapsing and lying still. Without another look at him, Philip grabbed the telephone receiver from its cradle and dialled the Morrison's number. The telephone was picked up almost immediately.

"Yeah?"

"Alan? It's Philip. Look, don't hang up on me, mate. I've been round to Howarth's. He's let the story out about all of this."

He realised he was speaking to a silent line. Alan must have broken the connection almost before he had begun. He stood for a moment in frenzied thought before rushing out of the house and jumping back into his car. He gunned the engine and the car shot away from the house, forcing it into a tyre-squealing turn in a driveway beyond before setting off back towards the village.

As he raced up the cul-de-sac, he saw that the curtains were still drawn across the Morrison's house. He ran his car into the drive and rushed up to the door. He rang the bell repeatedly before knocking on the door and finally shouting through the letter box. As a last resort, he tapped on the windows, but this also drew no response from the house's occupants.

A flash of light from the garage caught his eye and, through the small glass panels in the door, he saw that Alan's Passat was still parked there. A flicker of movement from the kitchen windows caught his attention and he turned to glimpse

Pamela's tear-streaked face staring out at him. As soon as he moved towards her, she snatched the curtains shut so violent that one hung loosely from a broken track. Anger and rage slowly metamorphosed into concern and worry as he returned to his car and drove slowly away down the cul-de-sac.

When he arrived back at the garage, he snatched up the workshop's phone and tapped Dr. Clarke's number into the keypad. The connection was made almost immediately and the phone rang once before it was answered.

"Dr. Clarke? It's Philip Bellamy here. I was wondering if you'd seen the newspaper yet?"

The psychologist's voice was loaded with sarcasm.

"The newspaper? I most certainly have seen the newspaper, Mr. Bellamy and I am as mad as hell about its contents."

Philip drew a deep breath in an attempt to calm himself before continuing, hoping that his would also appease the psychologist.

"Look, Henry, I've already dealt with Howarth. He was the one who let the story out in the first place."

"I knew that as soon as I read the ridiculous claptrap. Don't forget it was your idea to involve the man in the first place."

"I thought that having his word might count for something. You yourself agreed when I said that we might be able to keep tabs on him better that way."

"This is correct. But I am not near enough to watch him all the time and you have quite obviously not done what you said you were going to or this would not have made the papers. Do you really think that a man like that would stand by his word? People like that have no code of honour, they don't know what trust or honesty is. In fact, judging by the contents of this news article, I don't know that they could spell the latter."

"All I can do is apologise, Henry. I had no idea it would turn out like this."

He thought that the psychologist's voice softened a little.

"Apologies aren't any good here. I have a reputation to keep and being quoted out of context in a rag like this won't do it any good at all. It was your responsibility to ensure that this was kept quiet until we had enough material to allow a sensible article to be written for a quality newspaper after the witnesses have given their permission. All I can do is write a report on the initial interview and my subsequent hypnosis session. After this, my involvement comes to an end. I don't want to hear anything else about UFOs or aliens or anything of the like. I had hoped that the field had advanced during my absence, but it is quite clear that you are still chasing your own tails. I'll do the report when I have a spare moment."

Philip began to speak but, once again, found himself talking to a dead telephone line. He replaced the receiver slowly and trudged up the stairs to the flat.

******

CHAPTER FIFTEEN

TIME TO LEAVE

Alan rested his hands wearily on the corner of the sink and looked out into a grey world as yet untouched by the rising sun. He turned slowly and looked at Pamela, who was sitting at the kitchen table, cupping a mug of steaming tea in her hands and staring wearily into its murky depths. He realised now just how vulnerable Pamela had become since their experiences. Lately, she had not spent a waking moment very far from some familiar and old source of comfort and she was becoming more and more introverted as the time passed. He felt an aching inadequacy within himself now as he realised he could no longer bridge the void of doubt and fear between them. He felt as if the time for reaching out had gone.

Without a word, he left the kitchen and went upstairs to wash and dress. As he passed the bedroom, he felt the silent invitation of the bed's warm comfort. He longed to climb back under its covers and stay there until death finally took him. The day seemed to stretch out ahead of him like a rugged grey wall of insurmountable rock.

When he returned to the kitchen, he was surprised to see that Pamela had not moved. He leant over the table and gently took the cup from her hands. She looked up at him with the pleading eyes of one about to lose her last grip on the one thing which kept her from falling into the dizzying chasm below. He held one of her hands and sat down.

"Come on, Pam. We've got to go out there and face it. It looks like they've all done the dirty on us now, so we'll have to work things out ourselves."

"But, why would Philip do something like that?"

Alan's eyes darkened.

"I don't know exactly why he did it, but I'd bet my last quid that he's a bit richer this morning. Come on now. You go and get dressed and get Wendy up. I'll make a bit of breakfast and then take you off to work. She can come with me to school."

Pamela continued to look doubtful and insecure. The urge to take both of them away from it all was almost overwhelming. There had to be places far away from here where they wouldn't be known or recognised, places where they could start all over again, places where the events which had come to dominate their lives so quickly could be allowed to settle into their memories and become more and more vague as the passing years softened their experiences. He needed to exert himself almost physically to halt his train of thought.

"Come on, Pamela. It's going to be hard today, but tomorrow will be all the easier for facing it. Most people won't even understand what they've read, so maybe we still have the chance to explain our side."

"They'll know alright." She shook her head and wiped tears awkwardly from the corners of her eyes. "Come on, let's get this over with."

Alan spent time in silent consideration as Pamela dressed and roused Wendy. Her noisy descent of the stairs woke him from his intense thought and he looked at the clock with a start. He was going to be late again if he didn't leave soon. He began to prepare a hurried breakfast for Wendy as Pamela brushed by him and unlocked the door. She was outside for only a moment before she crossed the door's threshold shakily and sat down slowly on a stool. Wendy immediately left her own seat and ran to comfort her mother. She ignored her daughter's attentions for a moment and turned to Alan.

"Take a look outside."

Without a word, he stepped out onto the drive. He thought at first that someone had thrown a can of red paint all over the garage doors then he slowly realised that letters existed within the mess. As he moved slowly backwards, he entered the graffiti artist's perspective and the sentence resolved itself.

E.T. PHONE HOME!!

Surrounding this message were numerous other ones, smaller both in size and length, all relating to a particular section of yesterday's article. He ran to the garage doors in rage and threw them open against their stops, noisily rattling the driveway railings and causing a large crack to appear in one of the glass panels. He worked his way along the garage walls to the car and entered it with difficulty. After a moment, the engine barked into life and he slowly manoeuvred the large vehicle from the garage. He left the engine running and walked back into the kitchen.

"We'll shift that lot tonight. I'll buy some paint remover today in town."

Wendy's eyes lit up with cautious curiosity.

"What is it, dad? What's up?"

"Nothing, love. Get your stuff together and go and wait in the car. Put a tape on if you want."

"What's on the garage door, dad? I want to go and see it."

During the course of Wendy's life, she had been hit once and shouted at twice by Alan. He managed to restrain himself physically this time, but frustration fed the strength of the verbal order he delivered this time.

"Wendy, I won't tell you again. Get your things and get into the car. MOVE!"

Wendy shied away, as if she had been struck physically and even Pamela seemed shocked by the tone of his voice. Wendy's eyes filled with tears and her bottom lip trembled as she silently left the table and tramped up the stairs to collect her school bag. As soon as she was out of the room, Alan sat down heavily and held his head in his hands

"Shit."

Pamela looked on reprovingly.

"You can't take it out on her, Alan. It isn't her fault."

He brought his fists down on the table top with a bang.

"Whose bloody fault is it? We're out in the middle of nowhere and Christ knows what goes on and suddenly it's all on our doorstep. Why the hell does it have to be us anyway?"

Pamela raised her voice to compete with the volume of Alan's outburst.

"I don't know what or why, but I know it isn't her fault!"

"Don't you think I don't know that? If I could get my hands on Bellamy now I'd take his fucking head off as soon as look at him."

"Do you think that'll solve anything? The damage is done now. We're going to have to live with it."

Alan's voice became incredulous and he stared at her with wild eyes.

"Live with what? What the bloody hell has happened to us, Pam? WHAT THE BLOODY HELL HAS HAPPENED TO US?"

He stood and grabbed her roughly by her arms. She was shocked by the ferocity of his attack and struggled against his painful grip. He continued to shout, his face an inch from hers.

"Come on? How the fucking hell are we supposed to live with this? Tell me that, miss bloody practical? The papers are full of our faces; we've got that shit all over the garage and a crank UFO investigator with just about everything on sodding tape! What the bloody hell are you going to do about that, eh?"

Her own fear gave her strength and she broke free from Alan's grip, twisting her body away from him as she delivered a slap to his face which made his ears sting. He was stunned for a moment and noticed that her eyes were blazing with anger as his senses began to function again.

"Don't you ever do that again, Alan! Don't you ever touch me again! If you're going to lose control, then you'd better get lost now. I'll take almost any kind of behaviour but physical abuse from my own husband! Get out of here now! BUGGER OFF, ALAN!"

They both paused, captured by an unnatural calm, as they sensed another presence in the room. Wendy stood at the kitchen door, holding her school bag protectively in front of her chest. It was quite clear to both of them that she had seen most of the events of the last couple of minutes. Her eyes also burned with anger, but she said nothing. There was another long silence before the tension broke and they all rushed to embrace each other. Alan cradled both Wendy and Pamela's heads against his chest and spoke softly in an effort to calm them.

"I'm sorry. Both of you. I'm really sorry. It's just all getting too much for me. I don't know what to do. Maybe we can get in touch with the woman who did the article and get her to print a full retraction in next week's paper."

Pamela shook her head.

"That wouldn't work. We're big business now, Alan."

She glanced across at the telephone receiver which lay on the worktop out of its cradle, as it had been since yesterday. A light in the receiver's body continued to flicker periodically, indicating an incoming call on the line. There had been little peace since the story had broken yesterday. Alan chose to ignore Pamela's last comment. He was painfully aware of the truth in it. Instead, he parted himself from them and looked to the door.

"We'd better get going or we're all going to be late. Both of you wait for me in the car."

Pamela picked up her bag from the kitchen worktop.

"No. I'm going to get the bus and try and catch Janice before we get into work. If I can tell her the whole story, then I'll at least have an ally."

Alan looked at her for a moment and she registered his silent understanding.

"I'll see you tonight then."

She nodded.

"Tonight. I'll get a takeaway. I don't feel much like cooking."

"Okay."

He left with Wendy in tow. They both waited in the car until Pamela locked the house door and set off over the fields to the bus stop. Alan took one last look at the building which had become their one last source of security before he reversed the car off the drive and swung it onto the road.

As he drove to school, he noticed that the traffic was light and didn't realise just how late he was until he caught sight of the clock as he reversed into the only

remaining space in the school car park. They both left the vehicle's soft and protective interior and parted quickly, heading for their respective classrooms.

Alan arrived at his form room to find Brian Wilcox poring over the register and attempting to decipher the children's names. Silence fell as all turned to stare at him in surprise. Brian immediately picked the register up and walked over to the door. They both stepped into the corridor for a moment.

"I haven't got time to finish this, Alan. I'm sorry. By the way Potter's looking for you and he's got hold of a copy of your article."

Alan stared at the ceiling in frustration and shock.

"Look, Brian, you've got to understand that all of that was written behind our backs. The first we knew of it was when the damn thing came through our letterbox yesterday. I won't deny that something happened, but it was nothing like that. They've gone and blown the whole thing out of proportion."

Brian nodded calmly despite the situation.

"I know they did. You can tell from the way the damn thing was written. The only problem is that the cat's out of the bag now. This has already been bounced off the staffroom wall this morning and I've stuck my neck out to save you from a couple of slaggings. I don't think things will get any easier."

"I know, Brian. We're just going to have to stick at it."

He glanced at his watch.

"Yeah, look. I'd also keep Wendy out of it for a while. I noticed that a few of the kids in your form have got hold of the article as well."

Alan flinched as if he had been stabbed.

"Okay, Brian. Thanks for the warning. I'll try and nip this thing in the bud."

With the briefest of smiles, his friend handed the register to him and left. Alan braced himself and entered the classroom. The wall of silence which greeted him seemed to hold within it an undertone of alienating malice. He noticed that some of the children regarded him with critical eyes, whilst others refused to meet his gaze at all. What had been a happy and friendly classroom a fortnight ago was now a jury room holding thirty young minds, all willing to happily crucify him and strip him of his sanity with their brutally naïve childish logic.

He opened the register and began to call out the list of names. Each time, he received a curt response which felt like a small raindrop in the suffocating sea of silence. When the list of names was complete, he closed the book and stood to face them all. The bell jangled as he picked up a piece of chalk. The children reached for bags and began to move, but a shout from him knocked them back into their seats again.

"Nobody leaves until you are dismissed! Now pay attention to me!"

With the chalk, he slowly drew a flying saucer shape on the blackboard. Underneath it, he wrote the letters, **U F O.**

"I am sure that you all know what this stands for. A lot of you will already be associating me with this word. I saw that you had a copy of the article in question, Naomi. Would you be so kind as to bring it here?"

The chubby girl left her seat unsteadily and walked slowly and uncertainly to the front of the class. She gave him the crumpled piece of paper and returned

hurriedly to her desk. He unfolded it and stuck it on the notice board next to the blackboard.

He regarded it for a moment before taking a pen from his pocket and scribbling madly across the two pages. This had made him angrier than he had ever been in his life before He turned back to the amazed class.

“There is a word to describe this article which I have heard a few of you using in the playground. I won’t use it now because that would get me into a lot of trouble, but I want you all to remember that that is all it is. There is not a grain of truth in any of this and I don’t want you to tell anybody otherwise. I’d also like you to ask anyone who thinks otherwise to come and see me. Between Mr. Potter and myself, I’m sure we can break down a few stories. Now go to your lessons and tell your teachers why you’re late.”

The children filed out in stunned silence until only one figure was left at her desk. Alan walked over to her slowly.

“What’s up, Julie? Are you not feeling well?”

She looked up at him with troubled eyes.

“I read that article, sir. I think it’s what you said it is as well. It’s just that Naomi and a few of her friends have some sort of plan going. I think they said something about seeing Wendy about something this morning.”

Alan’s eyes darkened with concern for both Julie and Wendy.

“What do you mean, 'see her'?”

“They said they were going to ask her about the article, but you know Naomi.”

Alan nodded

“I do indeed. Thanks a lot, Julie. I’ll make sure that neither of you come to any harm. I would appreciate it if you could stick with Wendy through all of this, though. She’s going to need a good friend for a few days.”

Julie smiled wanly.

“I’ll do my best, sir. I’ll arrange to meet her every break.”

He smiled and gently knocked her chin with his knuckle.

“Thanks a lot, Julie. When you and Wendy get together this weekend, you’ll have to decide where you want to go and I’ll take you both out for the day somewhere. All expenses paid.”

Her face brightened a little as she collected her bags together and stood in preparation to leave.

“Thanks a lot, Mr. Morrison. I’ll see Wendy at break.”

She hurried through the door, leaving Alan leaning against the now empty desk. He had always been thankful for the period of free time which he always had on a Monday morning, as it allowed him to catch up with the piles of unmarked exercise books which always hung around the classroom. This morning, he abandoned his half-hearted attempts to work soon after the school settled down and lessons had begun. Instead he sat in unbroken silence and fought the almost overpowering need to sleep which had been with him now for over a week.

He must have drifted off in the warm silence, because the images came flooding back to him again, somehow less vivid and frightening this time than they had been before. He awoke to the sound of the school bell and looked at his watch. He had been asleep for over an hour.

As he stood up, a wave of nausea hit him and left a light-headed grogginess behind before it slowly subsided. He left the classroom and joined the seething throng of children heading for the school exits. He made slow progress, but eventually found the door of the staff toilets.

Once inside, he ran some cold water into a washbasin and threw stinging handfuls of it onto his face. As he towelled himself dry, he began to feel fresher and less tired than he had done for a while. His rising spirits were accompanied by a new sense of optimism. The insurmountable problem of the article now seemed less significant to him. He would confront them all and laugh it off as a huge joke. If there was one thing he could depend on within the school, it was the sense of humour of most of the staff. He almost began to see the funny side of it himself as he left the bathroom and headed along the corridor towards the staffroom.

As he passed an open window, he stopped as the sound of an unnatural playground struck him. He turned and his eyes widened in horror as he recognised the frightened figure cowering in the centre of a large group of children of all ages.

Wendy fought to free herself from her tormentors, but was viciously forced back into the circle each time she made a bid for freedom. She was aware of Naomi's voice very close to her left ear and it appeared that she was leading the verbal assault. She felt a hand take hold of her hair and then her head was yanked viciously back. She felt the left side of her face go suddenly numb and she realised with horror that she had been hit. A kick behind her knees sent her crashing to the ground and the sun was blotted out as the mob moved closer to stare at her weeping form. She was yanked suddenly to her feet by an older girl who screamed "Little alien bitch!" right into her ear before swinging her round and flinging her back to the floor again. Wendy regained her feet despite herself and turned to face Naomi.

"Leave me alone! Get lost, Naomi! Just leave me alone!"

She was pushed from behind again and then the circle began to jostle her roughly from person to person. A leg was thrust into the path of her headlong flight and she caught it with her right foot, the ground rushing to meet her. Her face was only an inch away from the hard, tarmac surface when a pair of powerful arms arrested her fall. She braced herself for the assault to come, and then found herself looking straight into her father's face as she was pulled to her feet. Without hesitation, she buried her face against his chest and began to cry hard. Alan turned to the suddenly silent mob.

"Every one of you will be punished severely for this. I have never seen such behaviour at this school. You're all a bloody disgrace, you disgusting bunch of animals. Don't you think I've got enough to cope with already, without you adding insult to injury?"

He looked round at the shocked faces within the circle for a moment before his attention was attracted by a mumbling from one of the older boys.

"No problem with aliens, though?"

Alan turned to him, his face flushed with anger.

"What did you just say?"

The boy backed away slightly, but his escape was arrested as Alan caught hold of the lapel of his jacket. He dragged him forwards until their faces were only inches apart.

"I asked you what you just said."

The boy pushed at Alan.

"Get lost will you! You're just as mad as she is!"

Without even pausing for thought, Alan swung his fist at the boy in a vicious arc which caught him just below his chin. The force of the blow sent him stumbling

back against the wall, where he stood for a moment, clutching his jaw in shock and staring at Alan with terrified eyes. Alan stared back at him for a moment with contempt before he turned to the rest of the mob again.

"Right, the lot of you disperse now! I'm going to count to five and anyone who hasn't left by the time I reach that number will be expelled immediately. NOW MOVE!"

They began to back off, stumbling over each other's feet in their haste to leave the playground. The silence which had fallen was suddenly broken by a shout from an upstairs window.

"Morrison!"

Alan turned to see the furious face of Sydney Potter at his study window.

"Get up here now!"

His face disappeared and the window was slammed so hard that he glass sang in its frame. Alan took hold of Wendy by the shoulders and pushed her tearstained face away from his chest. She looked up at him with fear-filled eyes as he handed her his car keys.

"Look. Go and wait for me in the car. I'll follow you in a moment. Don't stop to get anything or talk to anybody. Just go to the car and lock yourself in until I get there. Understood?"

She nodded.

"Good, now go on."

He ushered her away and watched her sprint towards the staff car park. He entered the school building through the nearest door and, with a determined stride, headed straight for Sydney Potter's office.

As he approached the door, he noticed that it was slightly ajar and he entered immediately after delivering the briefest of knocks. Potter's face wore a mask of sardonic amusement. His voice was little more than a sarcastic sneer. He gestured slowly to a seat which Alan sat down in slowly, never once allowing his gaze to break from the headmaster's face.

"It looks like the limelight has fallen on you this weekend, Mr. Morrison. I awake this morning and the telephone rings whilst I am in the bath. I answer it and find one of the school governors on the other end. He tells me about this article and I duly go and purchase the disgusting publication which contains it. I read it with interest, Mr. Morrison, and I am amazed at what I saw. I am intrigued by all of this. An explanation would be most welcome."

Alan's gaze locked on the headmaster.

“I wouldn’t say that every word was true, but I’ll vouch for the basic story told by the article to which you refer. A private investigation was being conducted by a number of people interested in this and it looks like one of them has sold the story. I had no control over the content, *sir*.”

The last word was loaded with as much sarcasm as Alan could muster. Potter seemed further infuriated by this, but managed to retain his unsettling calmness with an almost visible physical effort.

“How much did you get paid for this, Morrison?”

Alan took out his walled and opened it to expose a single five pound note and raised his eyebrows at the headmaster.

“If you take a fiver out of there, you’ll have your answer.”

There was an increase in tension and a tangible break in Potter’s self control.

“I have been amazed at your lack of respect for all but yourself, Morrison, but I never thought that your ego would carry you into such domains as this. You don’t appear to understand how much trouble you have caused me, Morrison. It would not be unreasonable to have you transferred in this case. I was thinking of somewhere where you couldn’t cause any trouble.

"For God’s sake! You have a responsibility to the children you teach and you have now made me question the trust I have placed in you. In short, Morrison, you’re a dropout as far as I’m concerned. The Dear Lord only knows what you were taking when you cooked all of this up, but I can only sympathise with your family in this case.”

Alan stood with unexpected speed, causing Potter to fall further back into the safety of his chair with a force which jarred everything in his ageing body. He fought his sudden fear as Alan leant across the desk until their faces were inches apart.

“Now it’s time for you to listen to me. In one week, I have been through more than you’ve probably seen in your entire life. I have sat here and had my intelligence insulted by you for the last time. You can take your damned tradition and stuff it where the sun never shines and you follow it with your bloody job. I’ll take myself somewhere where they don’t chain the kids to desks and make them learn their poetry.”

He turned as if to leave before spinning round as quick as a flash of lightning. The headmaster tensed in his chair again.

"And one more thing. If you were twenty years younger, I'd take your head off your shoulders for what you've just said about my family. Just pray that I never see you again outside of those school gates. I may just forget myself."

He left the room and slammed the door with enough force to rattle the bridge trophies on Potter's desk. He cut through the crowds in the corridor without a word and made his way to the car park. He gave Wendy a smile as he approached and motioned for her to open the door. He slid into the car's driving seat and kicked the engine into life. He slammed the gearshift into D and was about to move off when a shout from Wendy made him slam on the brakes. Brian had followed him, unnoticed, and he now banged on the passenger side window. Alan reached over and wound it down."What the bloody hell's going on, Alan? First I read that article and now Potter's hunting you down all over the school. Where the hell are you going?"

"We're all getting the hell out of here. If I don't bugger off to somewhere quiet soon, I'm going to end up bashing the shit out of someone."

Brian stuttered in disbelief and amazement.

"But... but when are you coming back? You can't just up and leave!"

"I can and I just have done. Potter can stick his job. Now let me get the hell out of here, Brian. It's driving me crazy."

Without waiting for a reply, he lifted his foot off the brake pedal and jabbed at the accelerator with such force that the tyres squealed in protest. Brian jumped back as the car surged forward and shouted uselessly after it as Alan steered through the school gates and shot off down the road leading to the village.

"Alan, you crazy bastard; where the bloody hell are you going?"

He stood for a moment, lost for a course of action. A familiar voice echoed across the silent car park and made him grimace. He turned to see Sydney Potter standing at the school's main entrance, his face red with rage.

"Wilcox! My office NOW!"

Brian set off back towards the school at his usual pace.

******

CHAPTER SIXTEEN

THE CASES ARE PACKED

Alan drove at breakneck pace towards the village, narrowly avoiding a number of collisions on the treacherous road which ran down the valley side. He ignored Wendy's squeals of fright as he powered through the village and only just made the bend onto the main road at its end. Despite her fear, she scrambled out of the back seat and sat next to Alan, pulling the passenger seat belt tightly around her.

"Where are we going, dad?"

Alan swing around a slow-moving Metro and accelerated past just as an articulated truck rounded the corner ahead of them. There was a screech of tyres and a brief flash of light before he swung the car in front of the Metro and sped on.

"We're going to pick mum up and then we're going to take a bit of a holiday. Don't you worry about school. I've got all the books you need for a while and I'll make sure you don't fall behind."

The road widened into a dual carriageway and Alan pressed the car's accelerator to the floor. The speedometer needle crept slowly up to and beyond the 100mph mark as slower-moving vehicles flashed past Wendy's window. She sat for a moment in contemplative silence before speaking again.

"I've read the article, dad. I've been having bad dreams as well, but I felt like I couldn't talk to you about it for some reason."

Alan snatched a quick glance at her before returning his attention to the road.

"It's okay, love. As I said, we're going to get away from here for a bit and then we can talk as much as we want. We're long overdue some time together."

Wendy's voice grew quiet and was edged with a childish uncertainty.

"I heard mum and you arguing. Are you going to split up?"

Alan laid a comforting hand on her knee.

"Of course we're not, love. Your mum and dad are going to be fine. Don't you worry about a thing."

He scanned the vehicle's instruments for a moment and saw that the rev counter vibrated into the red while the speedometer registered a wavering 125mph.

He instantly released his pressure on the accelerator pedal and became conscious of a mechanical crescendo from the engine compartment, which gradually decreased in volume as the vehicle's speed dropped to fifty miles per hour. He threw the vehicle off the dual carriageway and into a side road, fighting for control as it threatened to leave the damp surface at any moment. He careered on to his destination and brought the car to a screeching halt in front of the small office development where Pamela worked. He tapped Wendy on the knee.

"I'll just be gone a moment. You lock yourself in again and don't open the doors for anyone except me or your mum. Play a tape if you want, but don't turn the engine off. Understand?"

Wendy nodded and reached into the glove compartment. Alan engaged the locking mechanism as he closed the door and he nodded with satisfaction as Wendy secured her side as well.

He ran into the building and ignored the receptionist, climbing the stairs three at a time and sprinting down the short corridor to the closed door of Pamela's office. He paused for a moment as he heard raised voices, one of which he identified as Andrew Gibson's. Without waiting for another moment, he thrust the door open and

stepped into the office. Pamela was seated at her desk and Janice stood at her shoulder. They both faced Gibson, who had obviously been taunting Pamela with a copy of the newspaper article, which he was holding in his right hand. The scene froze for a moment upon Alan's entry before Gibson turned to him with a sly smile on his face.

"Hey, Al! What's all this about you and the aliens, then? I've been asking your Pam about it, but she doesn't want to know."

Alan did not speak but instead advanced towards Gibson in a manner which caused the smaller man to drop the article he had been brandishing and to move slowly into a corner. He flicked a glance behind him as the corner of a filing cabinet dug into his back and blocked his retreat further. He raised his hands and adopted a nervous grin.

"Hey... Al. No problem. It's just a joke, you know. What's up with you?"

Alan turned away and looked at Pamela.

"You okay, Pam?"

She nodded and wiped tears from the corners of her eyes.

"Okay, go and wait with Wendy in the car. I'll be down in a moment."

She began to protest, but Alan stopped her words almost instantly.

"Just move, Pam. Get your gear and go now!"

She folded the papers on her desk together and hurriedly shoved them in her bag before she stood and pushed her chair under her desk. Alan nodded encouragingly at her.

"Go on, wait in the car. I'll be right down."

Gibson took advantage of Alan's diverted attentions and tried to sidestep him, but was caught by his lapel and thrust against the filling cabinet by Janice.

"You hang around for a while, creep."

He stared at her, too terrified to speak, as Alan turned back to him.

"I'm going to ask Pamela just what you've been saying to her in a few minutes and I can assure you that she'll tell me the truth. If I don't like anything of what she tells me, I'll come back here and stuff your face somewhere where you thought it would never fit, you understand?"

Gibson nodded and pushed against Janice's restraining hand. She shoved the lapel of his jacket up to his chin.

"And that goes double for me, Gibson. I'm disgusted at you and I'm going straight to see Mr. Graham when Pam's gone. I don't think he'll be too impressed with you when he finds out why Pamela's gone. Do you?"

He was silent and avoided both of their gazes as Janice turned to Alan.

"Where are you going?"

"I don't know yet, Janice, but we've got to get away from here for a bit. I've got your address and phone number. Don't worry about us. We'll be in touch very soon."

She nodded.

"You look after yourself."

Alan smiled.

"I will. Thanks a lot for everything."

He turned and left. Janice released her hold on Gibson who sank into the chair which Pamela had recently vacated.

"That guy's a fucking nut."

Janice turned on him angrily.

"You shut your face. I've got a little report to write."

He stared glumly at his own unpolished shoes.

Alan followed the now-familiar route home, completely bypassing the site of their encounter and arriving at their house to find a number of strange cars parked in the cul-de-sac. The vehicles' occupants were obviously awaiting the family's arrival and doors opened as soon as they swung into the drive. One reporter snatched a couple of shots as they hurried into the house and locked the doors behind them. Alan parted the curtains for a moment to stare at them.

"That should make a nice little follow-up to yesterday's fairy story.

Pamela came up behind him and slipped her arms around his waist. He turned away from the window and held her close.

"Where are we going, Alan?"

"Strathclyde."

His voice was decisive. Pamela looked up at him.

"To your mum and dad's?"

He nodded.

"They can't trace me that far, so we should be able to get away from all of this there. It'll die down after a while and then we can begin to think seriously about what we're going to do."

Pamela contemplated their future for a moment and her eyes clouded with the uncertainty which had now become familiar to Alan.

"What do we do when all of this is finally forgotten, Alan? We still have to live somewhere and earn money somehow."

Alan's voice held a confidence which reassured her. It seemed as if he drew on a hitherto undiscovered source of inner strength which nourished him and dissipated the strain which the events of the past couple of weeks had placed on both his mind and body.

"We're both well qualified, Pam. We can get good jobs in just about any field with the experience we have. We can change our names without much difficulty and I'm sure that our faces won't be recognised after a while. We can start over again far away from here. We don't even have to stay in this country. Somehow I get the feeling that this may well be the break that we've been looking for. Wendy isn't old enough yet to have her schooling disrupted and we have no other real ties. There's nothing to stop us returning from time to time when things are quiet and visiting your parents if they'll still have us in the house."

Pamela laughed softly for a moment.

"I think dad will be having kittens about all of this."

Alan nodded.

"I could believe that. Look, we're going to have to pack stuff up now before we go. We can have the rest of the furniture moved into storage for now until we get set up somewhere. We'll sell the house by proxy when we have another place secured. Don't worry, Pam, its going to be okay.

She looked uncertain.

"I don't know if it is going to be okay, Alan."

He stroked her hair gently.

"Just you go and pack us some stuff and have Wendy do the same. Just use our three suitcases and let Wendy have the smaller ones in the set. We're limited to how much we can get in the car. I'll call mum and dad and let them know we're coming."

He released her from his embrace and she moved towards the stairs.

"Okay. We won't be long."

An hour later, Alan, Pamela and Wendy bundled packed suitcases into the car's spacious boot before quickly slipping into its protective bulk and speeding off down the cul-de-sac, shielding their faces from the prying cameras of the assembled journalists.

******

CHAPTER SEVENTEEN

DEAR PHILIP

As the weeks passed, the timelessness of the barren hills slowly seeped back into the little village and re-established order and calm, encouraging its inhabitants to return to their ways, some of which were as old as the hills themselves.

Philip Bellamy completed the case file on the Morrison's with meticulous care, as if paying his respects and attempting to atone for his errors. He visited their empty house regularly, as time passed, in the hope that they would eventually return, but he felt as if their departing was finally to be permanent when a notice appeared in the front garden offering the property for sale. As winter began to close in, he became aware that his beloved Triumph had suffered more from the ravages of a hard summer's motoring than he had ever imagined. It once more took up its place in the corner of the garage where he liked to think it went into a form of mechanical hibernation. There he lavished care and attention on its fine engine and gleaming bodywork, playing less and less heed to his waning interest in UFOs as the months progressed.

He rose early and dressed as the first snows of the winter dusted the landscape and he was surprised to find a small postcard depicting a bright summer scene lying next to a large brown envelope, both of which had been pushed carefully through his letterbox. He picked up the postcard and flicked it over to read the closely-spaced writing on the reverse. The signatures of the three Morrison's impacted with an almost physical force as he quickly scanned the message:

> Dear Philip,
>
> We arrived safely some time ago and we've not got ourselves set up here. We can't say where for obvious reasons, but we can say that it's every bit as nice where we are as where you are. Wendy has gone back to school and Alan's got a job in computers. The prospects seem so good and his boss says that he is a natural so it looks like we'll be set up for the future. We've found a good

mechanic so don't worry about our car – it's in good hands. We've got a BMW now, if you're interested. Moving back to the past for a moment, both Alan and I would like to apologise. We both know that it's not your fault now. You had no control over Howarth and you warned us of the risks involved. We were fools to ourselves. Nobody knows about us here and the article was never published in any of the papers, so we can only hope that the past never catches up with us. We have a good life now. I hope this finds you in good health and wealth. We'll be in touch again shortly. Once again, we want to thank you for doing your best for us. Without you, we would have all probably gone mad.

Alan, Pamela and Wendy Morrison. XX

He scrutinised the card closely for some form of postmark, but he had obscured any trace of one with a greasy thumbprint. He re-read the message then ripped the envelope open. Inside was a sheet of paper entitled simply *Psychological Report on the Morrison family*. It was from Dr. Henry Clarke. Philip began to scan its

contents, but came across numerous lengthy words which left him searching for a thread of meaning. He carefully placed the report back in its envelope and filed it with his own case report on the Morrison's. He placed his book on elementary psychology next to the two case reports and made the resolve to set aside time for interpreting Dr. Clarke's report. As he walked slowly back down the stairs to the garage, he felt the comforting weight of the socket wrench in his hand and he looked happily at the sleek shape of the Triumph in the corner of the garage. He didn't have much else on this winter anyway.

END

ABOUT THE AUTHOR

Philip Mantle is an international UFO researcher, lecturer and broadcaster. His books have been published in six different languages around the world. He is the former Director of Investigations for the British UFO Research Association and former MUFON representative for England. Philip has written articles and features for numerous publications around the world and has been both editor and assistant editor of high street UFO publications.

Philip can be contacted via his website at: philip.mantle@gmail.com
http://flyingdiskpress.blogspot.co.uk/

FURTHER READING FROM FLYING DISK PRESS

http://flyingdiskpress.blogspot.co.uk/

UFOs

CLOSE ENCOUNTERS
OF THE
FOURTH KIND
IN THE UK

MARK A. RANDALL / CREATIVE ARTIST
www.magcloud.com - cryptoriginals
www.magcloud.com - mark a. randall photography
www.welcometosleepytown.com

FLYING DISK PRESS

4 St Michaels Avenue

Pontefract

West Yorkshire

England

WF8 4QX

http://flyingdiskpress.blogspot.co.uk/

Milton Keynes UK
Ingram Content Group UK Ltd.
UKHW021412250923
429348UK00022B/414